# BLUE HERON
# CROSSING

©2013 James L. Ash

ISBN: 0615958591
ISBN 13: 9780615958590

For Linda Williams Allen,
my own river goddess, the love of my life,
for whom I will come back into the World as
many times as the World will let me.
Thank you.

# BLUE HERON
# CROSSING

# INTRODUCTION

This is a fantasy, a form that, it seems to me, is admirably suited to explore the "Real World". I have used many historical sources in these pages, notably the histories of Texas – of the war for Texas independence, the German immigrations of the 1840's and '50's, the Comanche wars, and the Mason County or Hoodoo War. I've even used the names of real, if lesser, historical characters because in the reading they seemed, naturally, to feel more authentic. There was a Thomas Grayson Mitchell, a John Floyd Gilbert, a Hoerster and a Wohrley, all of these and others in "real life" Texas history. None of them bears any resemblance to the characters in my fantasy, unless by divine accident. There was a real Mordecai Yell. I have visited his grave. Though, actually being a "circuit rider" in early Texas and so, obviously, an incredibly brave man, strong in faith, he bears no further resemblance to the character I have designed. I chose him for his wonderful name and the divine accident that led me to him.

The historical events I depict were real. Driven by my characters and my dramatic inspiration, I made very little effort to be fair or balanced to the parties involved in those histories. They are fascinating and heart-breaking and read like fiction. It is hard to believe that our forbears lived those lives and that so many of them survived to create this modern world and people it with all of us.

Speaking generally, the pioneers of early Texas seem to me, as a modern American, to be quite insane. Desperate for land and personal freedom, they put themselves and their families in harm's way carelessly. With only their faith and courage, they faced powerful enemies and died in great numbers. I have driven the course of the "Pinta Trail" across the Hill Country, following the paths of my characters. Even today there are huge distances with only blacktop highways and barb wire fences to show Man's encroachment. I imagine setting off across those open miles on horseback with no roads, only trails, and no fences, and it leaves me amazed.

Trying to be entertaining, I ignored the differences in language. The German immigrants spoke mainly German, especially among themselves. Even today there are strong German accents in those communities. Please do not hold me to account for that. I had no desire to invent some pigeon vernacular to tell my story.

Finally, I took little notice of actual geography in this story. The setting is the Hill Country of Texas. If you know it well you may discern the inspirations for some of the settings of my tale and decide it couldn't have happened that way in those places. They are only inspirations for the setting of my fantasy. Suspend your disbelief and join me at Blue Heron Crossing. Consider this an invitation.

James L. Ash
Wimberley, Texas
October 9, 2013

\*\*\*

*Music is the one incorporeal opening
into the higher world of knowledge
which comprehends Mankind but
which Mankind cannot comprehend.*

*Ludwig van Beethoven*

\*\*\*

# BLUE HERON CROSSING

## PROLOGUE

If you go looking for Blue Heron Crossing, don't drive the Texas highways. Don't try to follow the wide red lines and narrow blue lines and little black lines on the Texaco map you bought in San Antonio. You'll just get lost. If you go looking for Blue Heron Crossing, take the River. The River only goes where it has to go, so it always gets there.

If you go down the River, after it passes the interstate, after it winds past the mill race at Brady's Island, after the confluence with the Rio Claro, after the rapids at the Cotton Gin and its ruins, down past the low water bridge at Crocket Road, it comes at last to Morningstar and its dam.

Along the south bank of the river across from the town cemetery, lie 1500 acres of great pasture, bottom land all, rich and black and deep- a dirt farmer's paradise, except for the floods most springs... Because of that annual drowning, it's not the farmers but the ranchers who claim this place. Their crops have legs and can be moved to higher ground.

And on a bluff above the river past the first stock fence and the caliche ranch road, there sits a small house covered in corrugated sheet metal that long ago was painted yellow. It was built in the 20's to house a Mexican ranch boss and his family, but now is rented out to hippy slackers who came to the nearby city to go to teachers college. After wasting varying amounts of their parents' money, they have dropped out to be "river rats," as they call themselves, living on luck and short term jobs and drug deals. For twenty-five years they have passed this place down to one after another of their strange, disjointed family. They call it Blue Heron Crossing.

The origin of the name has been lost in the fog of time, in many stoned visions of the blue herons that frequent the shallows below the dam. The crossing refers to the low water bridge a hundred or so yards below the house. But when they sit talking far into the night, smoking their aromatic cigarettes and drinking whatever beer is cheapest at the time, they just call it the Crossing.

Across the dam is the small, near-ghost town of Morningstar. Back when cotton mattered the town thrived. Fourteen shops lined the main street. The state bank grew fat serving the farmers and ranchers of the area. Now the old brown brick buildings, one and a half or two stories high, are cobwebbed and empty, waiting for gentrification or a fire, whichever comes first.

The lord of Blue Heron Crossing these days is Grayson O'Bryan, called Gray, a sixth generation Texan, two of whose great-greats with 100 Tennessee volunteers, came to fight at the Alamo. Luckily for Gray, they arrived only in time for the Battle of San Jacinto. There, as any good Texan knows, Mexican General Antonio Lopez de Santa Anna and his troops were caught at their siesta. Seven hundred men were slaughtered. Santa Anna himself was captured while trying to escape dressed as a regular soldier. Gray's forebears were given 6,000 Texas acres for their part. Even after doling out the acreage to their troops, the holdings of Colonels John Floyd Gilbert and Thomas Grayson Mitchell were extensive. The only problems were the various tribes of Comanche, Kiowa and Apache warriors who claimed the area first, and the deadly dry and ruthless summers, and the impenetrable limestone ground of their holdings across the Balcones Uplift. And, oh yes, the already entrenched Texas government, already busy double dealing.

The story of the intervening generations is here represented by our hero. It is told in his flesh and bone and especially, his spirit. For every one of us is the sum of all who have gone before, creating us as they have created our world, as we create the world for our children and their children. Our children are, after all, our expeditionary force to the future, as we are for the old ones before us. Is it enough to say that Grayson Floyd O'Bryan is here, sitting on ground that once belonged to his family but has long been owned by others? Gray himself is not even aware of that fact. His mother might have told him if she had lived longer, but she did not. His father had heard it told once in passing but no longer remembers. Gray has no real past. He is a modern American. Yet bone deep, he is Texan.

But before his Texican forebears held this land, the Mexican people struggled here against the Comanche and the Apache. The Comanche took it from the Tonkawa and Karankawa. And before them, who knows? The land has been here always, standing outside of human concepts of time and possession. The land, and the rivers that cross the land, and the sea, they are the eldest, the absolutes, the eternal. They suffer us because they made us. They are our bones, and our blood. We are their children, their creatures. We pass through these hills like a song, echo a moment and are gone.

# THE WATERFALL

*S*he sang and she sang. *The summer was long in the world. August sucked at her substance, drained her energy. Her levels dropped alarmingly. Still she sang in her ten trillion tongues- highs and lows and all between. She was the loveliest soprano, the deepest bass. She had been singing this way for so long that she had sung everything, chorale masterworks of baroque fantasies, Gregorian chants, Mozart masses, Moon River, Snoop Dogg, barber shop standards, everything. She had her favorites, her best ofs, her medleys. Some might think that all she did were medleys, bits and pieces of everything all at once, too fast to comprehend. But, of course, that was because they listened from a static position in place and time. She didn't begin to understand these humans. She couldn't imagine their concepts of time and place. She had miles and miles of instruments and voices and she used them as needed to complete each of her creations. And time for her didn't exist. Or rather, it all existed at once. Or she existed outside of time and occasionally peeked in. A thousand years was unimportant. Millennia came and went, and still she sang. She completed the first movement of Beethoven's Fifth long before he wrote it. She didn't mind that he got the credit. She would have been glad to sing it to him, if he'd been around. Inspiring was what she did best.*

*The falls at the Morningstar dam were a favorite place for her. They offered a more dramatic range and tempo than her narrows and rapids. Naiad, goddess, elemental, muse, she had gone unnoticed for most of her existence. The old peoples who lived along her banks, they danced for her, prayed to her, sometimes brought her presents of grains and flowers, or pottery. These new people, they didn't know her at all. But that wasn't all bad. She wasn't as fond of them. When she went into flood she didn't have to worry about them like she did the others. Still, lately, since they built the dams at Morningstar, and other places along her length, she had begun to feel more sympathetic towards them. With their brief mortality they were almost as ephemeral as the mayflies that arose from her waters every year. They were totally reliant on time but not at all at home with it- moving from past to future as if they had a plan but really having no idea of what they were about... hapless. She laughed briefly, sadly, and went back to her song.*

*She was a goddess. She trembled with power. At times she walked the banks in beautiful aspect, blessing all that she met on her path. Occasionally she had taken a lover, some young brave or strong chieftain, but she was more careful now. She had nearly lost control once and that had been dangerous. Her heart was bright and alive and she feared becoming too enmeshed. She thought that love with a human was the only way she could lose her immortality and she was quite content to remain as she was. Besides, the mortals who loved her never seemed to fare very well after she left them. Broken-hearted, they wandered off to die in battle, or simply shriveled up and disappeared into death or some far country. Though she never gave them her heart, they were dear to her. Handsome and sensitive and young, or passionate and strong and brave, they all withered once she removed her grace. It was better not to play with them anymore, better for everyone.*

*Then one morning, below the dam, she saw him. He sat on a great limestone rock in the center of her course and he was singing...*

# THE HOODOO WAR

**H**ans Miller watched the four new riders fan out into the shelter of the live oaks on the ridge above the river. "Damn," he thought, "When things are bad enough they always get worse." That brought the total of the posse to nine. The rocks where he and Henry had taken shelter could be easily flanked now. Not that Henry would care. He'd been done for at least twenty minutes. He'd said he wasn't hit bad but that must have been the shock talking. Hans wondered what his chances would be that they'd take him back to town if he surrendered. Not very good he thought. Not judging from the way Random and his bunch had been acting up to now. He could see Random on his great black horse through the screen of the trees. He rode back and forth shouting orders. Every so often, it seemed to Hans that he might have a clear shot, but his target kept moving around too fast. The rest of the attackers were hidden in the shadows of the trees and difficult to see from his rocks in the bright sun.

Miller was part of a large group of German settlers who immigrated to central Texas in the 1840's and '50's. They had gotten ahead of the Texicans in the rush for the open land of the Hill Country. Many of the Texans had legitimate claims that preceded the German's- or thought they did. It was all politics and money and land impresarios and it had set the stage for the continuing bad blood between the two groups. During the War Between the States, as the Texicans called it, the Germans were fiercely Unionist which had caused more mayhem and murder. There were massacres of German conscientious objectors who tried to run to Mexico to avoid conscription. It was 1875 now and the anger had broken out into open warfare. The papers in Austin and San Antonio called it the Mason County War. But the people getting shot at called it the Hoodoo War for the evil spell that had turned neighbor against neighbor and had everyone hiding in their homes with their guns loaded.

Hans Miller and Heinrich Schuler had been returning from Fredericksburg after going to the bank there trying to raise money to buy a piece of land that lay between their two ranches. They thought if they could buy it they'd split it up between them. Didn't matter now, Hans thought, but the bank had turned them down. Things were just too unstable right now, the banker had said. Guess he was right, Hans thought. When they were still ten miles from town, Random and his riders had ridden to cut them off and the two made for the river. Why they were after them neither man knew. It was just how things were. But hiding there waiting to die seemed such a waste.

Hans wasn't afraid. Years ago during the War he had made peace with the fact that all men die. It was at the Battle of Bull Run. He'd been in New York trying to buy parts for a mill when Fort Sumter had come under fire. He was a new immigrant and very proud of his country. He was also a fervent abolitionist. The next day he'd enlisted. At Bull Run he came through two days of slaughter without hurt but nearly his entire company had been reduced to bloody death. At some point in the anguish and exhaustion, dying became acceptable. He'd never lost that feeling since, not through all the battles of the rest of the War, not through skirmishes with the Comanche, not through the many bar fights and the two gun battles he'd been in since he returned home.

The day they decided to come to Texas, Heinrich began calling himself Henry and insisted that Hans call him Henry as well. He'd been Henry ever since. They were best friends. They'd come to Texas together from the same town. They looked like brothers and on meeting them people often thought that they were. They were both tall and blonde and fair and good looking. Good German stock Henry said. They were in their early forties and would probably have been fat and florid by now if they had stayed in Germany and taught at the academy like they'd originally planned. They'd come to Texas to farm instead and they worked too hard to ever get fat.

Hans had been best man when Henry married his wife Sara. Sara was beautiful, the prettiest girl in the German communities. Henry was more than twenty years older than she was, and he thought his suit was foolish. Nonetheless he proceeded and was amazed when this young girl actually accepted him.

When he first realized that Henry was dead, Hans planned to go down fighting, taking as many of them with him as he could. That's what Henry would have done. Henry was hot-headed and fearless. When he saw the riders chasing them he had wanted to wheel around and charge them shooting. Maybe that would have worked better. Hans was more calculating. He went for the percentages. The percentages couldn't get past nine to two odds. Anyway, it was too late to change anything. It was done and Henry was lost. There was nothing left but the grieving.

Henry would have been for vengeance. But in the years since he returned from the War, Hans had become a follower of the Freethinkers, a group of German intellectuals who believed that reason should govern all human action. Vengeance never felt reasonable somehow. Henry was never reasonable. He got the two of them into one scrape after another. He did it in great good humor and laughed while he struggled. But once he lost his temper it all changed. He became implacable and furious.

One of the rifles had moved almost to a flanking position and was getting close with his fire. He knew time was short for him to act if he was going to. About twenty feet from the out-crop where he sheltered there was a slight depression that ran swale-like to the river. This part of the river was the Narrows, a cool and shady defile about seventy feet deep with fern-hung pools at the bottom. The area families came here on breathless hot summer days to picnic and swim. A series of small water-falls led to a thirty foot falls and a gorge… and perhaps his salvation. It was the reason they'd headed this way when every-thing started.

Miller fired a half a dozen rounds in the direction of the rifleman behind the live oak. Then he headed for the swale, dodging and ducking like a rabbit. He made it to the depres-sion and started crawling as fast as he could on his stomach, hoping that he was at least partially covered. Now it seemed a really stupid idea. There was no cover. They had to have a clear shot. To confirm his worries, a rifle bullet whizzed past his ear and ricocheted off the rocks ahead. He immediately jumped back to his feet and started running in a broken zigzag pattern. Nine guys aiming at him, nine. What a fool of a way to die.

The posse was shouting and laughing.

"Get him!" they yelled. "Don't let him get away!"

They were certain of their success. It might make them careless. That was his hope. And he thought he had made it. He was scrambling over the edge when the bullet took him. It went in over the right shoulder blade and he felt it pass through his body. Then he was pitching forward into the defile. His mind went into slow motion. He watched a great blue heron take off, startled at his coming. He saw the shining pool below rising up at him. He tried to put his arms up to break his fall and the pain in his shoulder blinded him.

He thought "I wonder what happened to my horse?" and it all went quiet.

# 2

## AUDITIONS

The morning was burning down as the Texas sun rose steadily up a pale blue sky, getting paler as it went. By mid-afternoon it would be nearly white, as August laid waste the summer hills. The Georgia cane at his bedroom window softened the light though, and consciousness began not unpleasantly... until he woke enough to move his head. Then the hangover announced its presence. It dragged his protesting attention from the dentist drill in his frontal lobe to the heaving wasteland of his stomach, only to be quickly intensified by the clamor invading the front room.

Arnie was obviously not in a good mood. Gray rolled over in his bed and looked at the clock.

"God damn it Gray, I told you to be ready. If we're late and lose this gig I will personally beat you to death with a tire iron."

Gray rolled to the side of the bed and sat up moaning with his head in his hands. "Damn," he thought, half out loud, "when things are bad enough, they always get worse."

But he said, "Keep it down for Christ's sake. Make some coffee while I shower and shave. Put my guitar in the car. And you'd need more than a tire iron".

He wondered if he could skip the shower and save Arnie some tension, but one glance in the bathroom mirror told him that would be a bad idea. His normally clear brown eyes were hollow caves hung with bloodshot spider webs. His fair complexion looked positively gray. He groaned at his own unconscious wordplay. His cheerful grin was now a frown of pain. His long, ash-blonde hair was already thinning and this morning looked lank and strangely shaped. Even his six foot frame seemed somehow shrunken and gaunt.

"No more margaritas" he said. "Never. No matter who wants me to drink them or what they offer." He could barely remember his late night passion anyway, if it even deserved that description. "Why do I do things like that," he asked himself. 'Why?" Then he climbed into the hottest shower he could stand and began the long road back to his recovery.

The gig was an audition for house band at a restaurant and bar called Caruthers's in the city. It was an upscale place that served steaks and seafood. The waits were nice-looking kids from the university and they made pretty good tips by being young and sexy and polite while serving the lawyers and doctors and real estate agents of the City. Being the house band meant playing every Saturday night in the bar. It was a good bar as opposed to all the really bad bars. There was no smoking inside, and the drinks were strong so the bands' tips were always good, and it paid $200 a night. And the clientele was more civilized and never got into fights involving pool cues, which can really damage musical instruments.

Arnie and Gray had been playing music together since high school. Arnie played bass and sang. Gray played guitar and sang. They were both songwriters and much of their material was original. The drummer had been playing with them since their sophomore year in college. Stanley was Cajun and difficult but he could keep a beat. Buddy played keys and they'd taken him on the year before to supplement Gray's guitar. Though it was harder to make any money when it was split four ways, it was sounding really good these days. They called themselves the Liberators, though they had tried many names before it and probably would try others. The most important part of the Caruthers's gig was that it lessened the pressure to book dates. Booking is the musician's curse. It takes enormous self-assurance to call club after club to find gigs. The new bar would give them a place to play every week, enough to keep them rehearsed and focused. They could still book more dates; but they didn't have to. It was an important distinction.

Stepping out the front door of the house was like being slapped in the head. The sun was ferocious and the late morning temperature was nearing a hundred degrees, but behind it, and around it, and through it was the sound of the waterfall... The Morningstar dam had been built in 1919 to power a giant cotton gin. Through the boom years it had brought the town prosperity and population. Now in its decline it was a ghostly, cavernous hall buried in shadows and broken machines sitting at the edge of the cemetery. But the dam kept roaring even in the drought years. It was about twenty feet high and its voice was a constant echo in the town... and behind every conversation and song at the house on the bluff across the river. Its roar was more plaintive than a roar should be. At times it hummed like a mother's lullaby. At other times it seemed to be a crowd speaking all at once- a big crowd in a cathedral or a railway station. Sometimes Gray thought that he could almost understand the conversation, but just as it seemed about to make sense it slipped away. Or he'd hear the shards of a symphony, brief but richly moving. He thought sometimes that all those translations were true, that every sound that exists in the world was dissolved in that rushing water. Sometimes he'd hear himself singing, a phrase from one of his songs, or, more exciting, a song he hadn't written yet. It never lasted long but if the words came with it he would begin to fashion the rest immediately.

Many mornings he would awake before sunrise and meditate for half an hour or an hour. He sat on a large limestone boulder below the dam about seventy-five feet upstream from the low water bridge. He sat and he watched the water plunge over the dam and he tried not to think at all. One February morning his meditation took him so deep that he found himself up to his neck in the river about twenty feet from his rock. How he got there he didn't know. As far as he could determine nobody saw him levitate, but (he'd laugh telling the story) it was early in the morning. At least he had no memory of wading through the icy river. Gray fought a serious inclination toward saintliness.

"You can't be enlightened," he'd tell himself. "Bodhisattvas don't have any fun."

The trip to the restaurant was almost completely silent. Arnie was pissed and when he was pissed he got quiet. This morning Gray was grateful. The ruins of his hangover kept jarring on his nerves as he went. But he knew Arnie could carry a grudge until the sun burned out, so he tried an apology.

"Hey man, sorry I wasn't ready. I got a little plowed last night." Arnie said nothing. "Sandy came over and made margaritas. You know how she is." Sandy was a groupie who'd been dogging Gray for a month or more. Arnie grunted.

"Anyway she jumped my bones and kept me up until after three. You know…"

Arnie looked at him with disgust. "Look asshole, this is an important gig. Not only is it fifty bucks apiece but it would be a great home base. All those doctors and lawyers, they have parties, you know? And parties pay real money. And who knows what else could happen? A lot of important people go there."

Gray muttered a humble agreement.

"And you don't need to be playing all hung over and shit."

"Hey man, I've played hung over lots of times. Sometimes I think I even play better. It puts me in the groove, you know?" Neither of them believed it. Gray was fumbling with excuses.

"So what's this party?" He knew but he thought it would be better if he kept Arnie talking.

"It's a free concert for some Rotary group's August birthdays. Stanley's buddy Hanover set it up."

There were two owners of the restaurant, both in their late twenties. The rumors about where they got the money to open their place covered almost all possibility, from drug running to lotto winners to an inheritance, to anything else the inventive imaginations of the town could devise. The one who did the booking was Rob Hanover. He'd heard and liked the band's CD, but he wanted a live performance. He wanted to know how they handled an audience.

After the band played an hour of mostly low key, pretty music for the over forty, over-fed members of the local Rotary, the party goers were happy and complementary. The tip jar held sixty-two dollars and Hanover was pleased.

"O.K. guys," he said with a confident smile. "You've got the job. You can start a week from Saturday. Two hundred a show, right?"

They all muttered their agreement and Gray shook his hand. The deal was made. Then Hanover smiled again. "So can I interest you boys in a little of the pause that refreshes?" That explains his confident smile, Gray thought. Cocaine always enhances your self-image.

Stanley said "Well, hell yeah."

Buddy said he'd like to but he needed to go. Gray wanted to leave too, only Arnie was his ride. Arnie was still too pissed to go along with Gray's schedule. He wanted to stay and he had the wheels. Gray didn't argue.

After they hauled out the equipment and instruments they went looking for the owner. In a luxurious office in an over-stuffed leather chair, Hanover sat and chopped up a couple of large rocks with a razor blade and started lining out rails. He was entirely too poised and successful. His shoes and clothes were perfect GQ. His Rolex glittered while he worked.

Cocaine is God's way of telling you that you have too much money, Gray thought, and told himself he was lucky not to have that problem. But Hanover obviously did. There was a mirror on his desk where snow was piled up against the heat of summer. Gray thought it would take a long time to melt.

It took longer than the musicians could spare, as it turned out, though their new employer seemed content to continue lining them up forever. Gray stopped after a single turn. That was all he needed to convince Hanover that he wasn't under-cover for the DEA. He didn't like cocaine. There were the obvi-ous problems with physical consequences that filled the paper from time to time. But mostly, it made him feel like he'd had too much coffee. He felt invulnerable, but the coffee jag feel-ing was miserable. And he couldn't write on it. That was the deal breaker for Gray. Writing his songs was the only important thing in his life.

Music was wonderful, especially when it took over and he lost his own voice. At times he would lose all consciousness of himself. It was like being inside the music. He would finish a song and realize he could never do it that well again. If he was playing for an audience they always responded as if they knew something different had happened. Those were the times people would come to the stage at the end of the set to talk, to thank him, to tell him they would be back the next time. When that happened he would realize that there really weren't any edges to the world. Everyone's consciousness overlapped. He would write songs that put him in another place, another person, but they would be as well known to him as if he had lived that life in that place himself. Once, after some trucker song, a truck driver asked him, "Who did you drive for?" and when Gray said he never had, the guy asked "So how did you know what it's like? Because that's it man. You got it".

The songs were coming further and further apart these days though. He wasn't sure why, but he'd begun worrying about it. Times were hard and that never helped. Trying to keep up with the rent and electricity and phone... not to mention eating and guitar strings, well, that was distracting; but he should be used to the starving artist thing by now. At night when he slept he dreamed melodies; actually he dreamed a melody, strange and beautiful. In his dreams he told himself he would write it down when he woke, but he could never remember it. He went over it in his mind until it made him crazy. It would come though. He just needed to be patient and keep trying. He'd go to the river. Sooner or later the inspiration would come.

## 3

# GRACE ANNE HAMILTON

He was on his way down Caruthers's wide and sun-bleached front steps when everything changed. He felt good. The job was theirs. The sun was bright instead of ferocious. The hangover had bowed to the superior power of the cocaine and he was still buzzing from the music. It had sounded great.

And there she was....

Her chestnut hair was short and curled around her face. Her wide-open eyes were an impossible shade of blue and widely spaced. Her mouth seemed about to smile even as she looked grim while ascending the wooden stairs. And her body made him want to turn around and follow her. That was the good part of coke. It always said you can do it. So he did. She was wearing sky blue short shorts with a pale blue V-necked t shirt and she wasn't wearing a bra. Her breasts were swaying and bouncing freely as she climbed and the V revealed a beautiful sun-warmed valley he wanted to explore. Her legs were long and slender and well-muscled and perfectly tanned.

At the restaurant's front door he moved around her to open it for her and she faced him as she went by and smiled. "Thank you" she said dismissing him. But he cleared his throat and looked back at her. "What?" she said smiling. When he just looked she said in an irritated voice "What... You've never seen a girl in shorts before?"

"No..." he said embarrassed, "I have; but I've never seen you before."

She rolled her eyes and walked away shaking her head, disgusted (he felt certain) by his stupidity. He stood there berating himself. He knew he should just leave. He knew he should, but he felt that if he left she would just disappear from his world as abruptly as she had entered it. And that couldn't happen. He couldn't let it, because in that first look into her eyes he saw lifetimes. He recognized love and betrayal, stories they would share, love they would make and children. He felt history profound and immeasurable and impossible to explain. In that moment, as laughably unreal as it was, he found a resonance that echoed off the stars. He had fallen in love, and he followed her back into the restaurant.

She was at the hostess station, talking to the manager, asking if she could get an application. The manager was a woman in her early fifties with bleached hair and a harried expression. Her eyes were busy taking in the short shorts and the braless look.

"No honey, I'm sorry but I'm not accepting anymore applications this semester. I have a full staff and a file full of names. Most of my people applied at the end of the spring semester. That's how I have to do it, to replace the people who are graduating and leaving town. Come back in December and we can talk." And she disappeared through the kitchen doors, leaving the girl looking disappointed, and frustrated.

Gray, feeling the courage of the cocaine, chose to seize the moment. "You could try *Lorien*" Gray said apologetically.

She turned to look at him angrily.

"What?" she said. "What is Lorien?"

He tried to smile disarmingly- "Lorien is a health food restaurant a couple blocks from here. You won't make as much money but you'd do all right. It's a much better place to work."

"Yeah? So why is that?" she said crossly.

"The people are nicer and the food is good and the yuppies go there so the tips aren't that bad. You should check it out. Besides, they're friends of mine and I know they need a waitress right now. And they won't care if you wear shorts to put in an application."

Now she was smiling and looking at him. Her angry expression had been replaced by one of interest. "OK," she said, "so who are you? You've got my attention."

"Who am I? Now that's a loaded question. How is a person supposed to answer that? My name? My name is Gray. I know. That doesn't sound like a name. It's a color. Still that's it. Short for Grayson Floyd O'Bryan. I mean, what choice do I have? Floyd? Get serious. OB? Please... Grayson? Sounds like a Victorian novelist. So Gray. That's it."

She opened her mouth to say something but his buzz could not be stopped. He didn't even slow down to take a breath.

"I'm a musician and a songwriter. I was born here. I'm twenty-seven years old. I've had three years of college in three different majors. I live on the river in a little town about ten miles from here. I'm an only child. My mother is dead. I plan to finish school one day- as soon as I can decide which major I want to follow. I'm shy and quiet unless I'm on stage... Um, I'll tell you more if you want but I'd rather wait until dinner."

She was laughing. That was good.

**4**

*Come forth Mist hair*
*Smoke hair, Mother of mine*
*Chaltchiuhtlicueye,*
*White Woman*
      *(Aztec goddess of rivers and water)*
*Aztec Ritual Poetry, Ruiz de Alarcon (1629)*

## WHITE WOMAN

Rain... singing... wind... beautiful... shadows... music... water... light... shadows... light... music... shadows... light... flickering... God the music... He swam up toward the light but it receded as he came and he was back, sliding down into the dark again... again... and again... He didn't know how long that went on but he finally made it all the way into the light and opened his eyes to it. He was in a cave and light was rippling on the walls of raw stone and a voice was singing a strange and beautiful lullaby. There were few words to the song. It was mostly melody and bliss, deep and undeniable. He lay on a bed of cypress branches, fragrant and green. And the disembodied voice sang on and on. Without words it said

"Shush, shush my darling. Everything is fine. Don't be afraid; you are safe. I will protect you..." Again he slept.

\*\*\*

There was a bowl of clear water beside his bed. He drank it and he slept.

\*\*\*

Twice more he woke to drink and sleep again. The third time she was there. She wore a simple deerskin shift and she was smiling. He had never seen anything beautiful before her. Nothing. His heart hurt to look at her. His world changed forever. All his definitions crumbled. When she spoke to him it came out as song, but she wasn't singing. She was just speaking. Her voice was low and full or tender and high and it took him a long time to realize that she was just talking to him. Like anyone would talk to him. She was conveying information, pausing for his replies, smiling into his eyes. He couldn't really tell what language she spoke. He understood it but it didn't go through the normal processes in his brain. She was very pale; no, not pale, her color was so light that she almost seemed to shine from within. Her eyes were as blue as morning sky in early summer. Her features were beautiful. And her hair was dark honey, a river of light. And, while she sat there beside him, the music grew louder and seemed somehow to become part of her dialogue.

His shoulder hurt, a deep, constant ache. It came back to him then- the chase, Henry, the Texicans. And then he began to understand what she was saying.

"How do you feel Hans? Can you sit up?"

Her smile was strangely distant but very warm at once. Nothing seemed real. He thought he must be somewhere hallucinating in a fever dream.

"You need to eat something. Are you hungry at all?" How, he wondered, did she know his name... and he slept again.

The next time he escaped the dark, she was nowhere around. He tried to guess how much time he'd lain there but he had no idea. The music was gone as well, replaced by the sounds of the falls. Maybe it was just a dream, he thought. And then he realized that someone had brought him here, bandaged his shoulder, brought him water. Falls, he thought, what falls? He tried to get to his feet then but the room swayed and spun. Sinking back, he wished for her, the girl, the woman, and as the world slid away again and he sank into the shadows, he heard the music filling everything with peace.

# 5

## DEWEY

He picked her up in his next door neighbor's old pickup truck. It had a bench seat and no AC and it smelled like stale Cigarillo smoke, but old Alonzo always let him use it after dark if he put gas in it. Alonzo's wife never rode in the truck. On their occasional nights out they drove a Lincoln town car. Alonzo was a black man around seventy years old, maybe more. He and his wife lived a quarter mile down the caliche ranch road in a nice brick house on an acre and a half of ground that he had bought years before from Mrs. Mitchell, the woman who owned the ranch. He also leased the rest of the acreage from her to run his cattle. Old as Alonzo was, Gray had never seen anyone work as hard. He was a typical Texas rancher- up in the dark, work until after dark. And most of the time he worked alone. Sometimes he would interrupt Gray's solitude to ask his help with some exhausting job. Once he'd had a trailer stacked sky high with hay bales that he wanted to get in the barn before the impending rain caught him. The barn was just across the yard from Blue Herron Crossing. The band was rehearsing and Alonzo was persuasive enough to overcome the whining of Gray's crew.

"This ain't work" he told them. "This is fun. Work is when you're alone and it lasts all day."

Arnie groaned. "So much for my childhood dreams of being a cowboy."

The old rancher laughed. "You city boys don't know about work. Come work with me awhile. I'll teach you. It's the best thing you could ever learn." And in a very short time he had them all laughing and moving together like it was a song they'd been playing forever. The band loved him after that and never minded if he asked for their help. That made for great neighbor relations for Gray.

Annie lived in Barrio Pescal, one of the old Mexican neighborhoods that the students had begun to invade because the rents were cheaper there. It was called Pescal because of its location behind the federal fish hatchery on the southern outskirts of town. She rented an apartment in one of the big old houses that had been cut up by some professor to make his fortune from student housing. It was a warren, but when she opened the door he walked into another world. Indirect lighting showed a room lined with overflowing bookcases. The few sections of open wall held pictures of wildflower-strewn meadows and river banks hung with cypress trees. There was music playing, Vivaldi he thought, and she was standing there looking so good that he couldn't speak.

"So where are you taking me?" she asked him.

She wore a close-fitting dress in many shades of blue. Its simple lines accentuated her lithe body. It was cut low in front and a necklace of topaz excused the stare he couldn't entirely control. He smiled at his date.

"I thought we could go to Lorien" he answered. " It would give me a chance to introduce you to my friends and you could talk about that job. Besides, the food is really good."

"You're a smart boy. I think I'll like that about you", she said, and she smiled easily, with just a hint of self-satisfaction. He had the feeling that he had done as she expected and intended. He didn't mind.

Lorien was a theme restaurant and the theme was the elven kingdom of Tolkien's Middle Earth. The posts dividing the rooms and sections were imitation trees, real in appearance. Fountains bubbled in lights in the center of the rooms and waterfalls tumbled down walls into streams and pools. Every window was a scene in stained glass of beautiful women in flowing gowns, and lordly looking men, with dragons or eagles or horses. All of it was rendered in high heroic style. Hardwood floors gave way to bright tiles and all of it together made a beautiful peaceful backdrop to the waiters and waitresses dressed in costumes of the Middle Ages. String quartets filled the air with gentle music.

"Oh yes", she said as they followed the hostess to their table, "this will be just fine."

Conversation was easy and bright. He talked about his music and his mother, about being a starving artist and about his three majors. She told him about majoring in music, her parents' disapproval of her working, her three sisters, her boyfriend.

"Well he's not really, but he thinks he is. I try to ignore him but sometimes I still see him. He's persistent and pretty persuasive. But he wants to control me, you know, and I don't do well with that. Still he's sexy and sometimes he's a lot of fun. Oh, I don't know, I should just break it off completely but he's not making it easy."

"So, should I be here? It's probably not a good thing to confuse the issue if you're still involved." Gray didn't want to say it but he knew it should be said. "I mean… if there's a chance you could make it work…"

"Not at all," she snapped. Her eyes flashed with anger. "I came to school here to get away from him. But he followed me and got a job. I've told him I won't move in with him, that I'm not ready for anything permanent, but he keeps coming around anyway. It's just difficult to end it."

"Is he abusive?" Gray asked. "Has he threatened you?"

"No, nothing like that. He's not dangerous or anything- just persistent. I'm getting tired of it."

"Maybe you should just tell him to take a hike." Gray asked helpfully.

"I think I just did." she smiled and put her hand on his.

It was a fine dinner. She had chicken in a buttery sauce with new potatoes and a salad. He ordered a pork roast on a bed of wild rice. Annie wondered why Gray had called it a health food restaurant. The food was delicious. He said it was as healthy as over-eating was likely to get. It was made from mostly organic ingredients, from as many local sources as the owners could find.

Hank was a townie who had gone off to study at the Cordon Bleu in Paris after high school. He had worked for a few years in New York and come home to stay. His family owned the largest and oldest real estate office in town and his parents were indulgent. They had funded his restaurant and could often be found sitting at a front table smiling proudly.

Beth was a philosophy major at the college when Gray was still attending classes. They'd gotten to know each other in an English class and had stayed friends ever since, probably because they had never dated. She'd said she was going with someone, and, though Gray sometimes flirted with her, she was clearly not interested. And he had liked her fiancé on sight. He often wondered why some people you meet are friends immediately while some perfectly nice people never seem to fit. Gray and the Liberators had played the restaurant's grand opening two years before and still played for special parties there at times. Normally though, Lorien didn't have a live band. There was no sit-down bar.

Annie and Beth talked awhile about food and waiting tables while Gray's attention was focused on his apple cake and French roast coffee. It was decided that she would start on the coming weekend on the slower afternoon shift and get used to the setup before she had to deal with the evening crowds. While she went to the restroom, Beth talked to Gray about his new romance.

"But you know" she said, "I really like her. She's different from your usual pending heartbreaks. Don't push this one too hard. OK? She might stick around."

As they left the restaurant laughing and talking, Annie stopped suddenly and said "Oh no!" almost under her breath. A man was walking towards them from the parking lot. He was large, and looked very intense.

"Hey", he said, stopping in front of them and looking at her.

"What are you doing here?" she asked him.

"Aren't you going to introduce us?" the big man said with an unpleasant smile.

"OK" she said "Gray, this is Dewey. Dewey this is my friend Gray. So what are you doing here?"

"Your neighbor said you came here looking for a job. I came to see how it went."

"It went fine" she said. "I got the job."

"That's great." He said. "We'll go celebrate. My truck is right over there."

"Thanks" she said quietly. "I'd like to, but Gray and I were just leaving."

"Well it was nice of him to give you a ride but I can take it from here" he said, putting his hand on her shoulder. "I'm sure Greg will understand."

She jerked away from his grip. "No actually, we're going to get a drink."

"Hey, I'm sure he won't mind if you go out with your boyfriend to celebrate. Would you Greg?" he said, moving in front of Gray.

"But you are not my boyfriend." Annie said. "I've already told you that I wanted space. Now I think maybe I just want it over."

Gray looked up into the big man's eyes. "Buddy, I think maybe you should just call her tomorrow and talk things over. But, right now, I think that you should leave."

"I don't give a fuck what you think, *buddy,*" Dewey said, and drove a killing right hand at Gray's head.

Gray's father had been light heavyweight champion of the Coast Guard when he was in the service and had insisted that Gray learn how to box. He'd taken to it pretty well and had boxed in the intramurals for fun when he was in school. He stepped out of the way and came in over the extended shoulder to deliver a hard right to the big man's jaw. He went down. Gray stepped back and waited.

"Christ… I think my jaw is broken." Dewey muttered from a sitting position.

"I doubt it…" Gray said "or you probably wouldn't be talking. But you might go get it looked at just in case."

He felt totally calm and unmoved, like he always did in a fight. He didn't quite understand why, but it definitely helped.

"And just so you know, my name is Gray."

# 6

## THE BLUE HERON

He watched transfixed as the early morning arrived on the river. It began with a few sparks of light down the center of the water that gradually grew wider and longer until the whole river to the east of him seemed to shine with its own light. All around, its banks were still deep in shadow as if night had decided not to leave and would make permanent camp on this singing stretch of water across the Texas hills. But the river, the river had her own ideas and was as impatient as a lover for the light. Then morning began to come to the sky and the darkness began to lose ground to the light. Grays, then silvers, then tints of rose began to rise up from the eastern horizon.

The sun was still slow in coming when he saw the blue heron. She moved slowly at the south edge of the water, wading the shallows near the bank. He'd seen her before, both early and late. She was beautiful in her patient grace, stillness given form. Her color appeared to be borrowed from the water, as if she were the liquid silver of water made concrete. Then her neck stretched out and she plunged her head into the swiftly running current and lifted high the wriggling sparkle of a fish. For a moment only, the form of the fish and the heron's head and neck made one slim line, electric with the dawn. Then the fish was gone and she was as before. He turned his eyes to see the sky; watched the rose climb along an edge of silvered cloud. When he looked back to the river the heron was gone.

Hans had watched the morning slide up the river from the east every day for a week, ever since he'd grown strong enough to climb up to the mesa. He knew that he should have left as soon as he found his strength but he couldn't bring himself to go. It was the woman. He felt that this moment belonged to some alternate world, some universe not subject to the grief and struggle that waited for him at home. He didn't know how long he'd been here but he did know he wanted to stay. He couldn't bring himself to leave her and when he spoke to her about her coming with him, she laughed as if the idea were ridiculous. He thought she might be a settlement woman, hiding from the Comanche after they burned out her farm and killed her family. There were many stories like that before the War. She could have lived here alone since she was a child. She wouldn't tell him how she came here. When he asked she would smile and walk away, kissing his cheek or patting him as she went by.

The limestone cave that sheltered them opened in the side of the Narrows about a hundred feet below the big waterfall. She never told him how she brought him there or why the posse hadn't finished him as he lay helpless at the bottom of the defile. And he wondered about the cave itself. The place the settlers called the Narrows was a sinkhole, a place where the river had tunneled underground to make a cave which then collapsed. There were some problems with the cave that bothered him. First, he had been swimming here twice before when summer was fiercest, with Henry and his family. He didn't remember there being a cave here. And the Texicans would surely have searched for him. This place was wide open and easy to spot. How did they miss it? It was all mysterious, but the greatest mystery was the beautiful woman who cared for him so patiently.

Throughout his recovery she had been there, not all the time, but every day. She was bright and funny. She made jokes and played pranks on him. But it was all lighthearted. She was never cruel. She had never been angry with him, only kind and helpful. At times she seemed like a child. When they swam she would splash him or grab his ankles as he swam and pull him under. Her laughter was bright and melodic and came easily. And she swam like no one he had ever seen.

He wanted her. The day before, he'd sat at the entrance to the cave watching her swim, naked and beautiful in the clear water. The image remained fixed in his mind until it became a torment. But that torment wasn't solely physical. In Germany he had been raised in a strict Pietist home. His father and mother were rigid and seemingly unmoved by the World around them. God had given them their paths to walk in this valley of pain and they would walk without flinching or complaining; but also without joy. Sex was the devil's snare. Hans had been raised in their image but when he reached puberty he began to struggle with physical desire. It was a hard struggle. He would battle valiantly and think he was winning, when a beautiful woman would smile at him or touch his hand and all his resolves would collapse in guilty desperation. He prayed night after night, always expecting to awake transfigured, remade, whole and pure and strong. But the next day brought only more struggle, more guilt.

But the Freethinkers taught that sex was natural and should be accepted as part of life- without guilt. He'd been trying to escape his upbringing ever since. Now looking at his rescuer he felt more overwhelmed than ever. She was completely natural in her nakedness and when she saw him staring she smiled cheerfully and waved, as if she had no idea of any impropriety in the situation. She seemed even to delight in it. She must have come here as a girl he thought, and grown up alone without people telling her that sex was wrong. Perhaps he should just take her in his arms and make love to her, but sometimes there was something so deep and strange about her that it stopped him. Who was she?

He remembered the musical sounds of their first conversations and the way he seemed not to hear her voice when she spoke, but had no trouble understanding her. He had written that off to the effects of the delirium caused by his injuries, and then he began hearing that music echoing down the canyon. It was a sound so full of longing and wonder that it seemed to reach into his center, opening him to dreams he hadn't known were there. Finally he understood that it was her song, her voice.

That evening she made him dinner around a fire built on the wide ledge in front of the cave. She broiled a large bass on a flat rock by the fire and she heated bread that looked like tortillas on the same stone. Her cooking skills were natural and accomplished though he had never seen her cook before. Usually she left him a bowl of a sort of soup or stew. It tasted really good and so far he hadn't grown tired of it. As she cooked she spoke easily and brightly about some of the things she had seen that day. The things she mentioned were simple enough but when he tried to remember them later he couldn't quite bring them into focus. He did remember the conversation he started when they had finished eating. He told her that since he was nearly healed and stronger he had to go back to the world and he asked her again to come with him. And as before, she smiled and refused.

"I am not part of your world" she said. "It would not be fitting for me to go there."

He stood up abruptly in his frustration. "What has fitting got to do with it?" he said. "You can't stay here alone for the rest of your life."

"But I won't" she said.

"You won't what?" he said.

"I won't stay here." She answered, smiling gently. "I'm only here because you needed me. You were hurt. Those others were going to kill you..."

"Yes I know. Thank you. You saved my life. And now I want to help you. Where will you go? How will you go?"

"I'll go anywhere I want. I'll just go."

"But you're only a girl. It's a dangerous world."

"No I'm not." She said smiling again. "I'm not a girl."

She moved around the fire pit and sat next to him and she cupped his face with her hands. Then she smiled and kissed him. He didn't know whether the smile or the kiss was more alarming. The smile was wise and strange and totally erotic. But the kiss proved beyond question that she was no girl.

# 7

# SHOOTING STARS

**W**hen morning came he was alone, but the passion of the night before was as present as the wind that stirred his hair. The smell of her was everywhere, like the smell of the river, deep and sweet and green- blue with life. The taste in his mouth was honey and salt. He had never before seen the sweep of heaven in a woman's eyes. He had never felt the electricity of his body stretched beyond the present moment and into some nameless, timeless zone out of reach of fear and physical limitation. Loving her was like a feather surrendering to the wind.

She had left him wild grapes and bread to break his fast. After his meal he found himself singing. He never sang, never. But song rushed like blood through his veins. Sometimes words came with the melody. Sometimes there was only the music. His singing startled the blue heron from her place beneath the cypresses down-river. She lifted into the air like an angel's shadow and sailed out of sight down the morning sky.

Moving to the edge of the rock he dove into the water below. The crystal transparency and cold brightness closed about him and defined the limits of his body, his joy. And then she was there, swimming beside him. She slipped into his arms like the water itself and clung to him as close as his skin would allow. The water seemed to support them, and soon he had no thought of the river at all. They made love weightlessly and once again he was lifted out of himself to sail down the fringes of his consciousness completely free and untethered. Later, remembering, he was at a loss to explain why they didn't both drown. Afterwards they lay entwined on a great flat rock in the sun and he was more completely alive and happier than he had ever been.

In the evening, as twilight slipped into darkness, they sat together around the fire eating a dinner of roasted freshwater prawns nearly the size of lobsters. Juices ran from the corner of her perfect mouth and down her fingers to drip onto her bare breasts. From nowhere she produced a jar of red wine, dark and strong. He had become used to strange events since he had come here but he had to ask her where the wine came from. She had a wonderfully innocent smile but it was betrayed by the sparkle in her eyes. They were still naked and the warm night air tingled on his skin as the breeze stirred ripples on the darkening water. Her strong brown hand moved up his leg from his foot and he became less and less interested in the wine. The fact that her intentions were obvious had little effect on their outcome. In the marvelous tangle of limbs and skin and emotions that was their lovemaking, he felt no shame at his nakedness and passion and again he was surprised. Her effect on his world was cataclysmic, profound, changing everything. Overhead the sky was alive with a meteor shower more amazing than any he had ever seen. He noted that, since he had awakened for the first time in her presence, the World was constantly mirroring her actions, their actions. He still had too many questions but he knew now that none of them mattered. He would be with her as long as she allowed.

In the early morning before the sun, he awoke to find her sitting at the water's edge looking intently downstream. He sat beside her and put his arm around her shoulders. The chill of the early morning vanished immediately at her touch.

He bent his head to kiss the nape of her neck and she turned to smile at him. It was a sad smile he thought, so he asked her if something was wrong.

"You told me before that you were healed and that it was time for you to leave." Her amazing blue eyes welled with tears.

"No. Listen…" he said smiling, "I was wrong. We can stay here if you like. I'll take care of you, build us a cabin. We can do fine. Don't worry; I'm not going anywhere…"

"No" she said quietly. "You were right. You need to go back to your people, your world. I need to take care of mine."

"Don't be ridiculous" he said. "I love you. And what world will you go back to? Where do you come from anyway?'"

"Ridiculous?" she said. Her eyes blazed with angry light and her skin was hot to his touch. He jerked his arm away as she leapt to her feet. Where he had held her, his skin felt as if it had been seared by live coals. He felt afraid. The hair stood up on his body.

"I am never ridiculous!" she said furiously.

Then she turned away and shook as if she shivered with cold. And something happened to the light or to his eyes… something. There was a rushing sound like a river in flood. She and the world around her seemed to intensify somehow, became brighter, stranger. Her skin grew lighter and became very pale, almost white. It appeared to glow from within. The air vibrated and shimmered like it does from a fire. It only lasted for a moment and when she turned back to him she was smiling again and she and the world had returned to a normal state.

She moved to stand before him again, smiling that sad smile. She put both hands on his arm. At her touch the pain was gone.

"I have become very fond of you Hans. I suppose it was taking care of you, protecting you. And you are a wonderful lover. If I stayed here I probably would come to love you. But that can't happen. My world is too far from your world in place and time and expectations. You must return to your life and I to mine. But I will think of you fondly, always."

He started to talk, to ask her to explain what she meant, who she was, what she was. But she turned away and walked to the river's edge and dove naked and beautiful into the water. Once again the light changed and everything intensified. It grew very bright and then darkened again. When his eyes returned to normal there was no sign of her. He thought "I wanted to ask her if she'd seen the shooting stars." And then he thought, "I don't even know her name." As he watched, the blue heron rose from the river before him and sailed away into the rising sun.

8

# MORNING MEDITATIONS

He sat and looked upstream at the waterfall. The lake above the dam carried a perfect reflection of the great trees that rose heroically along its borders. The cypresses and cottonwoods had already begun to transform into great torches of gold. It would be an early winter. There were few lesser trees along the banks. The many floods saw to that. They swept away all but the most determined of the new growth. The sun had just claimed the eastern sky and the earth wasn't quite ready to pay homage. An occasional breeze rippled the surface of the river, to remind that it was only a counterfeit, a reflection. Otherwise, the illusion of a double world was perfect and confusing, especially to a mind drawn far away in open-eyed meditation. Which world was real? Why not both? If every soul can live many lives in a lifetime, why should a world not encompass a perfect twin? Ideas moved through his head but he gave them no purchase and they moved on.

Gray was at peace for the first time in weeks. He had been so busy learning to love his new love that he had barely had time for anything else. He made sure that the music didn't suffer. He still worked his material every day and the band was rehearsing twice a week. The Saturday night house band gig at Caruthers's was doing very well. It had only been a little over a month since they started and already the crowd was building. Hanover was happy and Gray had renegotiated a contract: the band's pay was commensurate with the bar's income. If the house got better their pay went up. He felt like some music mogul. And the regular appearance led to other work, parties and conventions.

And Annie was a constant surprise. Learning Annie was the most fun he'd ever had in his life. He wanted to be with her every free moment. If he could he would be with her now, but she'd taken the weekend off to visit her mother in Houston. He was a little afraid that his name would come up in their conversations and he wondered what her mother would think of the idea of her daughter hanging out with a musician. But he had begun to have faith in Annie's independence. He doubted that her mother had any better luck telling her what to do than he did. And she seemed as happy with him as he was with her.

The only thing that had really suffered was his day jobs. He usually kept money coming in by working part time jobs as a carpenter. He had two friends he worked with. Usually that gave him fifteen to twenty hours a week. With the music that was enough to keep the bill collectors at bay. But he had said no too many times lately and pissed off one of his employer/ friends and he'd had his head full of Annie and blown a critical measurement with the other. But they were both old friends. He thought that he could get back in their favor eventually but in the meantime he was hurting.

Still none of that mattered when he centered. The world became simple and calm again. The dawn meditations he did had kept him sane through all his problems. As long as he meditated he could keep himself positive; as long as he kept himself positive things would work out all right.

He was dragged out of his meditation by the sound of a woman singing a simple melody in a clear sweet voice. He noticed someone diving into the lake above the waterfall. He only saw it peripherally at first but it brought him back to the world. In times past the falls were a favorite swimming spot for the neighborhood kids. But that was before they'd pissed off Alonzo by leaving the area a big mess one holiday weekend. Alonzo had asked for his help cleaning it up and Gray had listened to his growl about the decaying moral fiber of today's youth for two hours.

"You know it ain't the town kids. It's you darned city kids, your fraternity boys and sorority girls. They have parties down here and raise hell. I'm done putting up with it."

So for most of the last year he'd closed the swimming down. There had been some arguments but when Alonzo wanted you gone you left. He might be over seventy but he was 6'6" tall and his eyes could be harder than carbon steel. Once he'd had Gray go with him at night to run off a noisy party of drunken fraternity boys. Gray had wanted to call the sheriff but Alonzo had laughed at that.

"We don't need the sheriff son. These college boys aren't bad. They just want to act bad." He smiled broadly. "But I am bad, Gray. And you know son, I think you got a little bad in you too."

Sure enough, one big jock type did start to act mean but Alonzo kept staring at him and moving closer while he rhythmically slapped a piece of mesquite cordwood against his palm. The kid's brothers dragged him away still making noises like he didn't want them to but he didn't put up much of a fight.

So someone was swimming. It was early, not yet seven and someone had already ignored the no trespassing signs and climbed the barbwire fence and destroyed Gray's sunrise meditation peace of mind. He was about to get off his rock and go throw them out when the person came out of the water and climbed out on the oak limb that everyone used for a diving platform. It was a woman and she was naked. And even from over a hundred yards away he could tell that she was beautiful.

# 9

# RANDOM AND COOPER

Random mounted up on the big black and rode down to the Narrows. The others were already down there lining the edge of the chasm, rifles at ready.

"So did we get the son of a bitch?" he asked Cooper.

"I don't know. I guess not. There's no sign of him except some blood."

"Well hell, let's get after him. We can send McReady and Cope down to the bottom end to wait for him and we'll just climb in at this end and work all the way down. Meanwhile we leave a couple of boys up here to walk the bank. We'll get his ass."

"Yeah, I guess" Cooper said uncertainly, "but he's shot bad. He should be right here. I know. I'm the one got him."

"Hell man, he's German. He's probably too damn dumb to know he's dead."

With two others they climbed down into the Narrows and began looking for their missing quarry. After two hours of moving through an exhausting series of pools and streams they came out at the other end of the chasm and met up with McReady and Cope, having seen no sign of the missing prey.

They were all soaking wet, tired and angry- and very frustrated.

"So where the hell did he go?" Cooper asked. "Did he fly away or turn into a fish?"

"He's probably dead at the bottom of one of those pools." Random ventured. "I don't know. I do know I'm done looking for him. If he shows up again, we'll deal with him then." He mounted up and spoke down to the other men. "Me, I'm tired and dirty. I'm going to get a hotel room and a hot bath. I'll see you at Garnet's tomorrow."

Garnet's Saloon was a meeting ground for the Texican sympathizers in Mason. Cooper and Random and their group used it as central command for all their forays against their German enemies. Garnet himself didn't appreciate their business. Since the cavalry fort down the main road had been abandoned last spring, business had slowed down a lot. With the Texicans hanging around, the Germans had quit coming in and the Germans were much better customers. They were quieter and less troublesome, and they always seemed to have money. The Anglos were a more dangerous and unpredictable bunch and they tore things up a lot, at least this bunch of outlaws that were working for the ranchers. It also made him wonder if the hostilities might not come banging through the front door and destroy the place, and him along with it. He laid his hand on the barrel of the shotgun behind the bar for reassurance but felt none. The world had gone crazy. It was a hoodoo for sure. He wished for the ten millionth time in the last twenty years that he hadn't decided to give up whiskey when he opened this place. He sure as hell could use one right now.

The evening sun was in the doorway when John Cope came running in shouting for Random. Random was out in the privy. Cooper left his place at the bar and went to meet him.

"Christ, man, what the hell happened?" he asked.

Cope kept on yelling- "McReady is dead. That German bastard shot him off his horse. Damn near got me too."

"What German bastard"? Cooper asked.

"The one you said you got yesterday at the rio."

"Horse shit! If that bastard ain't dead he sure as hell ain't running around shooting McReady! I saw my shot take him. Either he's dead or he's damn sure down. So start over and tell me what happened".

"Well, me and McReady were riding in, maybe six or seven miles out of town. And we saw this freight wagon heading in too. We thought maybe we could make a little green so we pulled up on it, just to see what they was carrying. The driver was old man Friendly and the guy sitting next to him was that German... or his twin brother one. When he saw us coming he stood up and started firing a rifle. He stood up. He didn't duck. He nailed Frank with his first shot and I dropped down on my horse's neck and took off running. I swear he could've got me too. He just didn't."

"What the hell are you talking about?" Random asked. He'd come in and was standing inside the door listening. "So why didn't he then, since you seem to know."

"I'm not sure, but I think he wanted me to tell everyone he was coming."

"Are you crazy? I know he's German but he can't be that stupid." Cooper sounded disgusted.

"Maybe *he's* crazy. I mean he stood up to shoot McReady. I do know he could've killed me and he didn't and I been trying to figure out why all the way into town."

"Shut up you fool." Random said. "If he's coming here he's damn sure crazy, and he's also a dead man... if it's him."

Cope was pissed now- "I'm telling you it was him, wearing the same clothes, the same hat; and not shot or dead. And he's on his way to town right now in Friendly's freight wagon."

"Well then let's go meet the wagon." Cooper said smiling. "I guess I have a job to finish."

"The hell you say" Random barked. "It was you started this; sending us after the wrong damned Germans. Meanwhile, Hoerster and Wohrle are still in the game and raising a posse to come after us again. Let me take care of this guy and you go see what kind of crew you can get together to meet Hoerster. I'll take Cope and Anders and I'll finish this in a hurry. We don't need another lunatic at our backs. We have enough problems to deal with in front of us."

Random got his way like he always did. Nobody wanted to argue with him, even Cooper. He didn't look like much but he was blood thirsty as any Comanche when he lost his temper. Word was he'd seen his father die in a shooting, getting his brains blown away by a shotgun blast. Cooper said it must've done something to him, but Cooper understood. That was the reason he was in this too. It was the damned Germans killing his foster father that had him leave the Texas Rangers and come killing people instead.

While Cooper and his bunch headed west out of town, Random and his two went east toward the outskirts and the road the supply wagons came in on. He set up his ambush in the second block from the town limits. Cope was behind the façade on the roof of the abandoned stage building with him and Anders on either side of the street. They had only waited about a half an hour when they saw Friendly coming. There was nobody else on the wagon.

When they questioned him, Friendly said "the German fella'" had jumped down about five miles east of town. He said he'd picked him up walking just this side of the river near the Narrows. He said he had no idea who the guy was. He just asked him for a ride.

"Said he'd lost his horse. He was kind of strange", the old man said. "He kept asking what day it was and if I was sure. I told him of course I was sure. It weren't no mystery, but he kept asking like he didn't believe me. I finally had to show him my bill of lading with the date stamped on it."

Random decided that their lost quarry would have to wait. The three of them headed west to meet up with Cooper, wondering all the way if they were being followed.

# 10

## BEAUTIFUL SARA

**W**hen Hans walked through Henry's front gate between the two big live oaks his friend had loved, the full weight of his loss came sliding down on him like an avalanche. The murder of his lifelong friend nearly brought him to his knees. And the thought of having to tell Sara about his death was impossible. He began to weep and he didn't understand that either. He had been crying like a child ever since she left him. But he didn't weep, not ever. He hadn't wept when he told his parents goodbye, or when a friend died in his arms in the war. Ever since the woman had left him he had been different. He couldn't make sense of it. He felt hopeless and empty and the time question made him afraid that he had lost his mind. How could he return on the day after the attack? He tried to remember how many days he had been sheltered in the Narrows, but it was a blur in his memory. He could only remember four or five distinct days but it had seemed like weeks. And his wound looked completely healed. Even the scar had receded. Who was she? What was she? He remembered the fairy stories that his omi had told him as a child to put him to sleep, about river Nixies, and the Lorelei. But they were only stories. It was crazy. Maybe he was crazy.

The caliche road meandered through the trees for fifty yards and then came out into the house yard. When the place came in view he began to run. There were four buckboards parked in front of the house and a large number of saddled horses standing around the yard. Sara was standing on the porch talking to Jean Enders, one of their closest neighbors. When she saw him coming she ran down the steps and met him halfway across the yard. She was weeping uncontrollably.

"Praise God Hans, you're alive!"

It came out in between gasps of air as she sobbed into his shoulder.

"I was certain that you were dead as well. I thought they hadn't found you yet and that any time they would bring in your body on the back of a wagon like they did Henry. Oh God, Hans, what happened?"

Hans led her to the front steps and sat beside her. Everyone came out of the house to listen. They stood around in a close circle. Some put their hands on his back or shoulders to comfort him. They were old friends and neighbors. Many had come to Texas with him and Henry. They celebrated together and prayed together. They joined together for barn raisings and harvests. There were a few Anglos among the crowd but not as many as there would have been a year ago before the trouble started. He told her about the attack in ragged stops and starts. He knew he couldn't tell the whole story so he said that he had fallen as he ran for the Narrows and had knocked himself unconscious when he fell into the chasm. He said that when he came to, the gunmen were gone and he walked out to the road. Friendly passed by in his freight wagon and he flagged him down. When he came to McReady's shooting there were murmurs of agreement and approval.

Rob Enders yelled- "That's what we should do with all these animals. We need to hang them all."

Hans stood up and spoke in a strong, clear voice. "Never mind. I'll take care of them. I'll take care of them all."

They all began talking at once but he pushed his way through the circle and walked through the front door of the house and into the parlor, where his oldest and closest friend lay on a table in his best clothes with candles at his head and feet. He knelt at his side and spoke to him in a hoarse whisper.

"I'm sorry if I got you killed Henry. We should have done it your way. You never listen to me. Why now? Why this time?"

He put his hand on his friend's shoulder as if to shake him awake but the stiffness of the body was so alien, so strange, that he began to weep again. Henry lay there still, and pale, and quieter than he had ever been.

Hans realized that Sara had come into the room and was standing behind him. She put her hands on his shoulders to steady herself and he felt the vibrations of her weeping in her grasp. "Listen Hans. I heard what you said about the murderers." She struggled to control her tears. "You can't go after them. They'll kill you too. They're professional gunmen. Henry wouldn't want you to get yourself killed. What difference would it make? It can't help him."

He stood to face her. "No it won't help him. But it needs to be done. And I should be the one to do it. Henry's not the first they've killed. And they tried to kill me. Maybe they will again. Better if I go on the offensive so I have more control. Anyway, it doesn't matter what happens to me."

She looked up at him, her tears still running down her face, her long blonde hair disheveled and falling down her forehead. "But Hans, it does matter. I need your help. I can't raise the girls alone, not out here. I'll have to go back to my parents or even to Germany. That's not what Henry wanted. We dreamed of a new life for our daughters in a new world. The plans don't work without him. But if you are there to help me… I might be able to make it. We're family. You were always part of our family. We love you, all of us, the way Henry did. Please don't get yourself killed. I couldn't stand it." She turned and rushed from the room in tears .

The darkness in his heart seemed to pour out into the room. The shadows darkened until it seemed they would swallow the candle light as well. He sank to his knees beside Henry's bier and wept.

# 11

# THE SONG

By the time he got off his rock and reached the area behind the dam there was no sign of the singer. He stood looking out across the lake. A kingfisher went plunging through the trees, its staccato call reverberating down the world. Farther upriver a blue heron made its quiet way along the bank looking for breakfast. Otherwise there was only the excited chorus of cardinals back in the trees. He wondered if she'd swum across the river and upset a rookery. But he didn't think cardinals had rookeries. Still, they were obviously concerned with something. He could see a dozen from where he stood. They were flying in and out of the dense foliage. But there was no sign of her. So where the hell did she get off to? He started up the path beside the river. It threaded its way through a forest of oaks and cottonwoods and mesquite trees. Occasionally there was an opening to the river, some quiet cell where generations of kids and lovers had carved out their own private places. But none of them held any sign of a beautiful woman, naked or otherwise.

Later that day, as the evening came sliding out of the east, full of endings and weariness, he heard her again. The voice came soaring up from the river as he sat with his guitar, trying to capture her song from memory. It was a sweeter and more plaintive melody than he'd ever heard before. There were no words that he could hear, just vocalizing, trills and a strange kind of choral scat singing that sounded like Ella Fitzgerald doing a Gregorian chant. He started running but before he got very far the song stopped again. He knew that at the dam there would be no sign of her, no sign that she had ever been there- no wet areas by the river's edge, no clothes or shoes or footprints, nothing.

He wondered who she was, why she was out singing on the river in the near dark. Her song sounded lonely and ethereal, haunting. It echoed off the river banks and the walls of the old cotton gin. It gave the twilight a strange wistfulness which grew into an intense longing with no object. He considered going down to look for her, but he was certain that it would be another useless search. Perhaps if he was patient she would come to him... And then he found himself wandering the river bank watching and listening anyway. He stayed out in the dark for over an hour but heard nothing more of the wonderful song. At last he walked back up to the house and sat on the porch again, staring off into the dark downriver and longing, longing... Finally after midnight he went inside and tried to sleep.

Over the next week he heard the voice nearly every night and twice at his early meditation, but he never saw the woman. Annie thought he was losing it. Somehow she was never there when he heard it, though she was there a lot. Parts of the song sounded strangely familiar, but he couldn't remember where he had heard it. It continued to produce a vague sense of longing in him, but he got better at resisting it. Most of the time he only listened and waited, but a couple of times he found himself out in the dark again at the river, listening and waiting.

One morning, sitting at his meditation, he tried to define his longing but he found the meaning just outside of his ability to comprehend. It was akin to the homesickness which he had felt when he first left Germany... he stopped and thought," Germany? Where the hell did that come from? I've never been to Germany." All through the day it kept bothering him, the way a dream does if you're trying to remember it. It was right at the edge of his mind but it wouldn't quite reach. But that night in his dreams he was on a ship, a sailing ship, and a man he seemed to know was speaking to him in German...

\*\*\*

## The Singer

*From the shadows above the dam she watched him. He was sitting on his rock oblivious to the world. His mind was far away in some quiet place. Once she had picked him up and dropped him in the current as a prank, but it was all much more serious now. Since she'd realized that it was him, her heart had refused her control. She watched him all the time, as he meditated, as he worked with the old black man, as he played his guitar alone on his porch. He sang such sweet songs that at times she had to harmonize with him. She tried not to because as soon as he realized she was singing, he would stop. He would get up and walk toward the dam, his head pivoting right and left searching for her. She wasn't ready to show herself to him yet.*

*She watched him completely unnoticed, smiling at his earnest searching. He was always so committed to any task. It was one of the reasons she was so fond of him. That focus was what had made him such a good lover. She was pleased to see that he hadn't lost that trait. When she had first realized that it was him singing on that rock, she couldn't believe it, but neither could she doubt it. The veils of dream were not part of her world. She recognized the real the same way she recognized the color blue. Either it was or it wasn't. She knew he didn't remember her. She was only beginning to understand the human journey. She had thought because they knew death that they were mortal. But they weren't. Their immortal spirits took a broken path. They went from one story to another, always on the stage of time.*

*It was strange that she hadn't understood that.*

*That evening she sang for him again as he sat on the porch at the house drinking a beer. The wind was in the trees, singing harmonies to the songs of the waterfall. It was one of her favorite moments. She raised her voice, clear and sweet, and as she sang for him she realized that she loved him.*

*It was as certain as the breeze rippling the surface of the water. It became part of her and made itself known in her heart. "Now what shall I do?" she wondered. "What must I do now?"*

*And then she knew.*

\*\*\*

## Heron's Wing

*The heron moves slowly, high overhead, a monogram of grace drawing the imagination along the silvered seams of the morning clouds. The earthbound watch with envy the impossible freedom of the sky. But the heron watches the river, the long shining thread of her existence, the promise of her hope, the other half of her sweet freedom.*

*Where is she going on this bright day? Her river is twelve hundred miles long, and anywhere in all that anteroom she can feel comforted, or follow the silence of her hunger, the future of her passion. And yet, with eyes as full of present and of past, colliding in a vision out of time, she searches all the tributaries of the infinite river of light.*

*She is the archetype, the prototype, the mother. As the feathered clouds ripple at her passing wings, the silken waters ripple far below. As the stars sparkle, far beyond this day, her eyes are full of light beyond the stars. Beyond time, still she creates in time. And in this moment, outside of time, she is weaving the thread of her soul into the temporal fabric of human life. Up the river to its source, the deep springs buried in the stony, beating heart of the earth, and down the river to its mouth, pressed against the endless, eternal sea, and back again, and back again, and again. Each transit sinks lower than the one before. She leaves the high and pressing clouds behind her far above. But with her, as she falls, she brings eternity, with a reach beyond even the ferocious, distant stars.*

*It is love that calls her, draws her, lures her- love, the singular expression of the living heart of creation. For love do the stars explode into being. For love do their cinders spin around them and sweat out oceans and raise up mountains. For love do they awake to life and breath and pain and death- for love only.*

*She does not know what she is doing. She hopes, certainly, but she does not know. It seems a beautiful theory, full of balance and belief, lovely in its logic. But she doesn't know. She does know that she will die. That much she is sure of. But what is death in the face of love? Still, how will her choice effect the eternal in her? She only hopes. She sings in all her many voices and she plunges singing into life.*

*A baby cries...*

# 12

## ANNIE

It was a bright and cool October morning, a Saturday morning. Gray was feeling good. The band was playing tonight. He made coffee while Annie woke up slowly from her dreams, like she always did. He wondered what she dreamt but she'd never tell him, even when she talked in her sleep, even when she sang. When she talked he could never understand her. It sounded like a foreign language, but one that he'd never heard before. When she sang it was fascinating and beautiful. Still, however vocal her dreams, she always said that she couldn't remember them.

In the morning Gray always made the coffee and brought in the paper. But today there was no paper. They were at the Crossing. Gray didn't read it, and they wouldn't deliver on this side of the river anyway. Annie read the paper every morning. When they were in town, he read the funnies and the weather, only wanting to know what Prince Valiant was doing and whether it was going to rain. Otherwise he couldn't think of one thing that he could help or hurt by knowing or remaining ignorant of the ways of the world- except his peace of mind.

But Annie seemed fascinated by everything, from international politics, to the arts, to the lives of the beautiful people.

He'd been talking with Hank and Beth the night before, telling them about her. They'd gone to a concert of early baroque music by the university orchestra. Annie was playing harpsichord. It was intermission and Hank asked how the relationship was going.

Gray smiled. "Life is music. It's like a Mozart wind concerto. Just when I think it can't get any higher and sweeter, it does."

Beth smiled and patted his arm lovingly, her brown eyes misting up. "I'm so happy for you, sweetie. I was beginning to think you were going to turn into one of those jaded, cynical musician types, going from one night stand to one night stand, Saturday night groupie to Saturday night groupie."

Hank grunted. "Oh yeah, tough life. I've felt so sorry for you over the years, wandering from Saturday night groupie to Saturday night groupie, blonde to brunette, to redhead. Having to meet a new crop of coeds every fall; always searching for that Mozart wind concerto and ..."

Beth elbowed her husband in the ribs, hard. "You watch yourself bucko, or you'll be searching for a lot more than a wind concerto. Seriously Gray, it's so nice to see you happy. You're always smiling now, every time I see you. And you seem to be getting a heck of a musical education as well. I've never heard you use a Mozart analogy before."

Gray laughed. "Well, you understand why. Annie lives music. She practices for hours every day, playing her piano, or her harp or her violin. Actually, I think maybe she really can play any instrument. I wouldn't be at all surprised to find out that she's a virtuoso on the didgeridoo. When I say her versatility is amazing, she tells me that music is all she'd ever studied. She went to schools for the arts all of her life and was always in the GT music programs."

"She told me that she went to Julliard for a year and left." Beth said.

"Yeah. She decided that she didn't want to stay in big cities anymore- the sirens and homeless and everything." Gray sounded mystified.

Hank said "I know what she means. That's how I felt in Paris. She should try it in another country where she doesn't understand the language."

Beth smiled. "Well honey, it wouldn't be in Paris. A French couple was in the restaurant the other day and she translated for them. When they left they thanked me for the excellent service and told me she spoke like she came from Provence. They also left her a twenty dollar tip."

Gray was still shaking his head. "I mean … Julliard. She walked away from Julliard. I told her she was crazy, that it wouldn't look good on her résumé that she had left Julliard to go to a state school in Texas. She just laughed. She said that she didn't care about a résumé. She said she could play in any orchestra she wanted to, or teach at any college, if she wanted."

He didn't tell them the rest of the conversation that he'd had with Annie about Julliard, but he smiled at the memory.

He couldn't believe that she could just walk away from the best music school in the world and he kept going on about it. Finally she smiled and said "But how else was I going to find you?" and when he asked what she planned to do when she graduated, she'd put her hand on his cheek and said "Well, we're still figuring that out, aren't we love?"

The lights were flashing and intermission ended. The three friends returned to their seats and let the harpsichord and oboe, viola and flute take them back to the seventeenth century for another hour.

The music was still going through his head as he stood looking out the window waiting for his coffee to finish perking. It was beautiful on the river in the chill of early morning. The mist drifted over the bright reflection of the lightening sky as far as he could see. Then he went out to the porch with his coffee. He had started to take Annie hers, but she was still sleeping and she wasn't working today. She usually took the day off following a concert, so there was no reason for him to wake her at all. He stood at the bedroom door listening, but the only sound was the soundtrack of her dreams. She was humming or vocalizing a phrase from last night's concert. It was the same line that he'd been remembering, something from Bach.

As he stood watching the light spill into the day from over the edge of the world, he realized that the music playing in his head and Annie's dreams was also coming down the river out of the predawn darkness to the west. It was the singer again, very faint and far away. He sat down on the porch swing and listened to the mysterious voice harmonize with the voice of Annie's dreams, and he wondered.

## Intermezzo

*Down the perfect hills and up she runs, singing. Will he catch her? She smiles. The cataract plunges in sprays of color, falling through emptiness forever. There are no colors like this. The melody roars and increases in intensity. Her song soars, higher and sweeter, calling to his longing. She smiles. His longing is greater than he is.*

*She is in the spray, in the pool below the falls. She is naked and glistening. The roaring waters explode into beautiful fragments of sound, of color, a fractal expansion of the waterfall and the dream. Here is the underlying promise, constantly growing away in an endless curving arc, at once ephemeral and concrete. She smiles. The kettle drums throb louder. The ocarinas swell ever more frantically. Oboes and bassoons gain prominence for a moment and then submerge in a whirlpool of melody.*

*What is this need that haunts him through the translucent hallways of sleep? What is this melody that carries him like a vessel caught in an irresistible current? It seems to be lust, like hunger-wanting; but it is more. It is subtle and multi-layered. There is passion for her, but passion for life as well, and passion for love, for creation and completion.*

*She smiles. He looks down the bottomless drop to her brilliant form. He is afraid. She smiles and he dives. She smiles... and he is falling and falling and falling... forever...*

# 13

# THE FAREWELL

**H**ans watched as Sara's wagon turned onto the road and vanished into the dust of the summer drought.

Then he went inside and began the letter. "My Dearest Sara," he began and searched for words to say what he had to say. However he said it, it would hurt her. In the end it would just be goodbye.

It was nearly a year since Henry's death. He had stayed away from the battles that continued to rage across the Hill Country. He had promised Sara that he would and he had kept his promise. He had tried to stand in for his friend with her and her children. He had worked Henry's farm right along with his own from before first light and into the night for months, but the drought wiped out all their efforts. Sara was going to spend the rest of the summer with her parents in New Braunfels, a German settlement east of San Antonio.

She was traveling with the Mitchell's, a Texican family who had remained faithful friends through all the months of turmoil. Tom Mitchell had been a friend since Hans and Henry had joined him in a fight with a Comanche raiding party twenty years ago. He'd been alone and getting the worst of it in a dry arroyo west of Fredericksburg when they'd heard the battle and come riding down out of the hills out-shooting and out-shouting the Comanche. They'd sent them running even though the three settlers were still outnumbered. Since Henry's murder, Mitchell had grown tired of the Hoodoo and decided it would be safer for his family if they returned to Nacogdoches where he owned another ranch. He had a lot of property in east and central Texas but he loved the Hill Country and was a man who relished his adventures. The legends said he had fought in the Revolution and was given a lot of property by the government. He brought a regiment from Tennessee, they said, and some of the Texicans called him Colonel. Hans even heard that Mitchell had rescued Sam Houston himself when he was shot and had carried him to sit under a tree until the battle ended. He thought it might be true because Mitchell would never speak of it or of the Great War either. Still he had a family now, he said, and the need to keep them safe was paramount. They would escort Sara and the girls to her parents on the way, which gave Hans some peace of mind. The girls loved it because the Mitchells had three kids, two girls and a boy. The girls all got along well, and together had a great time making Tom's son miserable.

Before they left, Tom Mitchell had taken him aside. He offered him his flask, filled as usual with Tennessee rye whiskey. Then he started in on Hans, like he had the last half dozen times they'd seen each other.

"So, what the hell is going on with you, boy? Why are you letting that girl go off to New Braunfels without you? If things are that hard, I can help out. I'd be glad to. If it wasn't for you and Henry I'd be nothin' but bones in a gully and a scalp on some Comanche's war lance. There ain't nothin' you need that I got you can't have, man. I thought you knew that. We been friends a long time now."

Hans mumbled his gratitude.

"Don't give me that stuff. I ain't your preacher, though I might say you could use one, you damned heathen. The thing is, that girl and those babies, they need you. You know what Henry would say. I don't have to tell you. His girls, they need you. And what's more, you need them. Maybe you don't know that yet but it's obvious as pain."

Mitchell had a way of talking you into a corner and not letting you out until he was damned good and ready.

Hans tried to argue. "Tom, how can I go on living Henry's life while his murderers are still running around free and unpunished and killing innocent people? It's been nearly a year."

"You know Hans, I'd like to think it was about Henry, but we both know it ain't. If you don't want to tell me what's wrong then keep your secrets, but killing yourself chasing those worthless bastards that killed Henry won't do any good. I'd say whatever it is, you just need to get over it. Life is only ours for a minute, to live and learn from, and the only important things to learn are love, and kindness, and courage. When you get older, like me, you start to see what's important. You should marry that pretty girl and get over whatever it is that's been killing you. Wake yourself up!"

And then he settled the luggage and his charges and started the long ride to East Texas.

Hans thought about what Mitchell said but he couldn't help but think that he was bad for Sara. He would stick with his plan. He would remain here and see about selling the stock so there would be some money at least for her and the children. Whether or not he would sell the farm as well remained undecided. Sara was strong and determined. She was not the woman to give up on anything. The dream she and Henry had nurtured for their daughters' future remained a link to her dead husband that was very much alive. She agreed to take a break and visit her family 'til the drought ended, if it ever did. Then, if things got better, she would buy more stock and start over. But Hans was tired. There was a weariness that had settled deep into his bones and blood that would not fade, whatever his stubborn will demanded. Part of it was the physical exhaustion of endless hours of hard work without a reward. But he could deal with that. He had been a farmer for a long time. Part of it was Henry's death. Though he told himself that it wasn't his fault, he couldn't shake the question of his decision to make a run for the river. Over and over in his mind he played back the memory of the attack. He heard the shouts of the Texicans as they rode toward them from three directions, Henry's cursing and spinning to the attack toward the weak side of the trap. But Hans had shouted "Come on! We'll head for the Narrows". And without waiting for an answer he had turned his horse and spurred him. And Henry had followed and died, shot from behind.

But even that wasn't really the problem. He could not escape the memory of the song, her song, her body, her mystery. At night he heard her call to him in a voice filled with music and longing. He saw her waving from a river alive with light, her nakedness reflecting the morning sun. He felt her in his arms. The longing became the most real part of his world.

Then a month ago, after he had worked an impossibly long day, first at his place and then at Henry's, Sara had convinced him to sleep in the barn instead of going home. In the middle of the night he awakened to her arms about him, her head against his back. For a sleep-blurred moment he thought it was the river woman and then he felt Sara weeping and realized what was happening. He turned to her and held her against his chest while she sobbed out her grief and loss. He murmured consolation and stroked her hair and shoulders. Then she was kissing him and moving against him and the comforting became passion and the passion claimed them both. Afterwards she struggled angrily back into her nightgown and ran from the barn weeping. Though he called to her, she fled to the house and slammed the door. Filled with guilt and shame he had saddled his horse and ridden for the Narrows.

Under an emaciated white bone of a moon he hobbled his horse and stared into the arroyo. He watched as the morning came trembling up the river like a promise whispered in a lover's ear. He called to her. "Where are you? You. Goddess. Woman. Whatever you are. Where are you?" He climbed down and searched the banks near the place he thought he'd fallen but she wasn't there. He wandered down the entire length of the Narrows calling her. The cave was gone, as if it had never been there. No trace of her remained to comfort him, or even to prove that it had really happened. If he could understand it, then maybe it would be better. This way he felt he was still caught up in a dream. Nothing seemed real, and caring about anything was almost impossible. And now he felt guilty about Henry and Sara. It was more than he could manage.

And the music, the song, her song- he was singing it constantly. He couldn't help himself. He woke with it in his head and it filled his dreams at night. Sometimes it would have words and sometimes he would just vocalize, but however it came, he was singing it whenever he was alone.

He and Sara had taken the children to the Fourth of July Festival in Fredericksburg. He saw a Mexican playing a guitar on the street and he bought his guitar for far more than it was worth, while Sara watched him like he was crazy. Since then he had played it every spare minute, teaching himself as he went. He bought an old music book in German that explained a lot about music but nothing about how to play it on a beat up Mexican guitar. Mostly it taught him how much of his first language had been lost since he'd left Germany. Still he made progress. But he made no progress at all with his memories.

Now that Sara and the children were gone, safe in New Braunfels, he could do what he had wanted to do since Henry's funeral. He could lose himself in vengeance. The world was a cruel theatre and the human dramas were meaningless and empty charades. He would pay back the debt he'd owed Henry ever since the river woman had cheated him of death. He would find Random and Cooper and the rest and end the battle. It was past time.

# 14

# MIDDLE OF NOWHERE, TEXAS

**"I**'m telling you, it would solve all your money problems." Stanley was talking about a job a friend of his had available. He was trying to help Gray out of his always present money woes. "Listen to me; the guy knows what he's doing. He has like, thirty fireworks stands." Stanley was the kind of guy who knows everyone. He could connect you to someone to handle any circumstance, fix any problem. Lately he'd set himself the task of getting Gray's finances in order. He wanted Gray to take a job at one of his friend's stands.

"He says you could make up to five thousand dollars- in less than two weeks. Can you come up with that kind of money any other way you've heard of? In two weeks?"

Gray wasn't crazy about the idea. The thought of spending two weeks on the side of some lonely road somewhere freezing… "So what about the music?" he asked, almost hopefully. "Who'll run the place while we're playing our gigs?"

Stanley smiled his "gotcha" smile. "That's the best part. We don't have any gigs. Christmas Eve is Saturday. The restaurant's not open. New Year's Eve is Saturday too, but they're having some big dance orchestra remember? Iggy Pop and the Royal Sumerians or something. Those are the only two possible conflicts. None of us got off our butts to book anything else."

Gray was almost ready to concede. "But we promised Beth and Henry that we'd play their party on New Year's Day."

Stanley was disgusted. "Hank and Beth are two of your best friends. They'll understand. And besides, boudreaux, you close up at noon on the first. The music doesn't start until four. You can make it."

So it was that Gray found himself freezing on the side of the road at the southwest corner of the intersection of RR 1705 and FM 166- the middle of nowhere Texas. Eight miles east down a worn blacktop highway there was the quiet hamlet of Hector; five miles west over a worn blacktop highway was Norton Springs. Somewhere out there were Austin and San Antonio and civilization, music and good food and Annie. He had borrowed a tent and a small electric heater for the tent and on really cold nights he could bring in the electric radiator from the stand. It would be ok. He would survive. That and a radio, what more could a guy ask?

Stanley had borrowed his brother-in-law's old Toyota pickup for Gray to drive. Both the registration and the inspection sticker were out of date and he hadn't had insurance for it in years. "Just don't have a wreck;" was Stanley's only comment.

"in two short weeks you will be on the way to economic health and prosperity." And then Dewey showed up.

Dewey Harwell Dawson, Annie's erstwhile boyfriend, pulled up in a big red Ram Charger with a camper on the back. He set up another fireworks stand across the intersection, catty-cornered to Gray's fireworks stand. "Damn it" Gray thought, "I knew it. When things get bad enough they always get worse." His mind quickly reviewed the number of cars he had seen in the four hours since he got there to set up, times the hours he would be open every day, times the amount he would make off of the average sale, times the twelve days he would be open, and then he divided it by two fireworks stands and he got a definite sinking feeling just south of his liver. "I am going to murder Stanley."

A plastic grocery bag flew past his face like a shabby, run-away balloon and hung itself up on the thorny branch of a mesquite tree some fifty feet away across the road. There it stayed, tethered and flapping in the wind like a wounded bird.

"Christ!"

# 15

## WAGNER

There was no trouble for a while. After Dewey's initial grimace of recognition he ignored Gray and Gray ignored him. The fireworks business was busier than Gray's original estimate judged it. Somehow between two towns with a total population of twelve there were hundreds and hundreds of boys between five and twenty. Add to that all the fathers who had to outdo their neighbors' fireworks displays on New Year's Eve and business got pretty brisk at times. And then there was Mr. Wagner.

Mr. Wagner was a strange, wizened, smiling old man who showed up the first night and spent an hour going between the two stands. Eventually he stood at Gray's counter and ordered over a thousand dollars' worth of rockets and mortars and aerial barrages as well as assorted crackers and chasers and bombs. "Your stand has better prices" he confided. "And I like you better too, son. That other fella is kind of sullen."

He told Gray to call him Wagner and said he owned a big ranch on the other side of Norton Springs. He'd been a geologist in the oil fields before he retired and he "made a killing, son; made a killing." Now he sat on his ranch and got bored unless he was traveling. He'd been everywhere for his work, and every place he'd liked, he'd gone back to since he retired. He had no family, but the Mexicans who worked for him on his ranch had lots of kids and they loved fireworks almost as much as he did.

He came every day in the dead part of the afternoon and he always brought a thermos of coffee laced heavily with Irish whiskey. He'd pour out a cup for himself and one for Gray and he just talked. He'd stay as long as his thermos had liquid to pour and he talked while Gray stocked shelves. He talked about the strange places he had been and the memorable people he had known and the things they had done together. Some of his stories were hysterically funny and some were heartbreaking, but they were all fascinating. His spoke in a strong, clear voice that could rise to a cackle when he was describing some ridiculous scene or tremble with a deep foreboding whisper when he related a tragic ending. If customers stopped he waited patiently, but those moments were rare enough at that time of day. When he left he always took at least a couple big grocery bags filled with bright and shiny explosives. After a couple visits Gray began to look forward to his arrival. One day he didn't come until almost midnight when the stand closed.

"One of the kids had a Roman candle blow up in his hand", he explained. "I had to take him up to the emergency room in Fredericksburg. Oh, he's all right, just a bad burn. He'll have a good story to tell at school is all. His main worry is that his mother won't let him shoot off fireworks anymore. But I told him, give her time, she'll come around". Maybe because it was night, Wagner brought a bottle, as well as his thermos. They sat in lawn chairs and drank and talked until after two in the morning. As the conversation quieted toward the end of the night, Gray told him that he appreciated his business and his whiskey.

Wagner said "It's great to have somebody to talk to son. You know, Gray, sometimes you meet people and you just know you're going to be friends." Gray agreed. "I think the reason for that is that you've known them before. You understand? In some other life."

Gray asked if he really believed in reincarnation. "Sure I do" Wagner answered. He said he'd worked a lot in India and all over Asia. "Nobody doubts it there. Their societies are based on it. Think about it", he said. "Wouldn't that explain a lot?"

Gray admitted that it would but said that it would also raise a lot of questions. "I don't know Wagner. It seems to me life is complicated enough without esoteric explanations. I just try to hang on to the things I know are real."

Wagner nodded his head. "Well son, that's a good idea, sometimes. But you know, in the end what is real and what you think is real may have absolutely nothing in common."

He tossed off the last of his coffee and groaned his way to his feet. "Anyway boy, I believe it. I think we were good friends before and, more important, I think we're good friends right now." And he climbed into his truck and drove away.

# 16

## MORE THAN AIR

When Christmas Eve came the crowds got heavy. Why the crowds came out on Christmas Eve he could not understand, but come out they did. Gray's main rap that night was worrying about Santa getting shot down by all the rockets. Every night he had some joke or topic of conversation that he used with all his customers and honed as the night went along. Annie had come out to stay with him and bring him his presents. She had decided not to go home for Christmas and that had melted Gray completely. The fact that she would rather spend Christmas Eve working a freezing fireworks stand with him and sleeping in a tent amazed him. She could be at her family mansion in Houston's River Oaks with her parents and sisters, and no doubt receive all kinds of expensive presents. And he knew her folks had not been happy about it. He'd watched her face from across the room when she told them on the phone that she wasn't coming. But she was happy. She hummed under her breath as she filled orders and every little boy that she waited on fell in love with her. "Just like me" he thought. That was when he decided to ask her to marry him. "Not right now", he thought, "but when I get it a little more together."

Wagner came and he got a chance to introduce them. He was pleased to see that they liked each other. Whenever there was a lull they were busy talking away. Wagner decided that they would all have Christmas dinner there tomorrow. He would bring the food and they would sit down together "like a family" he said. Gray and Annie said that would be wonderful but he shouldn't go to so much trouble. He said "Don't worry, Angel is already making dinner. I'll just have her make an extra set. We always have a big dinner for all the folks on the ranch- every Thanksgiving and Christmas. There are four families living there and it gives us a chance to learn how everyone is doing. Some of them have kids who have kids. It's really more than four families, because the kids are welcome to stay if they want to work on the place. A few do, but most move on." Angel was his housekeeper. Gray wondered how Angel would feel about that and decided it that it really wasn't his business.

At midnight, when the stand shut down, Wagner made his goodbyes and walked to his truck. Annie was worried about him. Had he had too much to drink? Was he sleepy? Gray thought it strange, since as many times as they sat drinking Irish he had never even thought about it. But Wagner assured her that he was OK and that it was Christmas Eve night and the roads were deserted. He'd be just fine.

Since the temperature was supposed to go down into the teens Gray took the precaution of moving the stand's radiator into the tent. After he'd finished closing up he walked out to the tent, some fifty feet behind the stand. It was glowing green from the light inside. The canvas fluttered in the wind. It was a beautiful and completely romantic vision. Annie was playing his guitar and singing a Christmas carol, sweet and clear and high. When he opened the tent flap and came in he was stunned by the loveliness of the scene. Annie sat on the covers over his double sleeping bag. She had changed into a soft white flannel nightgown. She was barefooted and her hair was brushed out in a soft cloud around her face. She was singing a madrigal, in Italian he thought, and as she sang she smiled the sweetest, purest smile that he had ever seen. The tent was surprisingly warm. He had laid old carpet in two layers for a floor and put a windbreak canvas over the whole tent.

He sat by her and put his arm around her and before he even thought about it he said "Annie darlin', I love you more than air." She laid her head against his shoulder and he said, "Will you marry me?" He hadn't meant to say it. He'd never told her that he loved her before. It was still too soon. He had nothing to offer her. He was a struggling musician. She was a rich man's daughter. It was insane. But he meant it and he didn't regret saying it even in the first shocking moment of realization.

And she smiled and hugged him one armed. "You know that you're crazy! But of course I'll marry you." And that was it. His life was settled. And beyond any understanding he loved it.

# 17

## GIFTS

Christmas dinner was delicious. Evidently Angel was a hell of a cook. Gray wondered how Wagner stayed so skinny. They ate on the card table that he did his accounts on. It was a very cold Christmas. Their conversation rose in clouds of steam above the table. The menu was turkey and dressing, mashed potatoes and a big fruit salad. There was pumpkin pie for dessert. Hot coffee washed it all down and warmed their blood, especially after Wagner added his "special ingredient". The turkey was small and they managed to make a good showing. They ate in the early afternoon and were occasionally interrupted by customers- usually boys whose parents had been talked into braving the cold against their better judgment. But everyone was filled with Christmas spirit, including, unfortunately, Annie. She decided that since it was Christmas she should take a plate of their dinner across to Dewey.

Dewey had been staring bleakly across at them for two days. Annie felt sorry for him because he was alone at Christmas, and he seemed to have far fewer customers than Gray did. She walked across the empty intersection smiling and talking, wishing him a merry Christmas and holding out the plate. Dewey met her at the door to his stand and knocked the plate from her hands cursing. Gray couldn't tell exactly what he said but his intent was clear. He vaulted the high counter and ran across the intersection while Wagner shouted for him to wait. But Annie moved in front of him and put her arms around his waist. He was furious but she kept saying "No, no darling, it's all right. Come on back." She held him and he stopped. He was looking across her shoulder at Dewey, whose face was a snarl of rage. He turned around with Annie and, holding her, he walked back across the highway.

The dinner party ended then. The magic Christmas mood was broken and seemed irretrievable. Wagner loaded up the remnants and got ready to leave but before he did he gave them Christmas presents. They were neatly wrapped packages in bright Christmas colors. For Annie he brought a necklace, a heavy golden chain with a golden pendant.

"It's an Egyptian cross of life, an ankh" the old man said. The upper part was a large pearl held in a golden loop.

Annie nodded.

"I bought this many years ago in Egypt for someone I loved. I was working in the Near East." He grunted. "But by the time I saw her again she didn't love me anymore. It means many things my dear Annie. It is a symbol of eternity" he said, "and of the union of man and woman and so" and he smiled "of conception. But you don't have to get in a rush." She tried to refuse, saying that it was too much, but he insisted. Then he turned to Gray.

"You remember I told you that we had met before?" Gray nodded. "Well, this came out of that conversation. I meditated about you. I was trying to see if I could uncover our connection but all I came away with was this." He handed him the gift and Gray took off the paper and held a small box. When he opened it he found a gold pocket watch, obviously quite old. "That was my great grandfather's. It doesn't work and hasn't for a long time. My father tried to have it repaired but they said it couldn't be fixed. It used to play music when it opened." Gray opened it and saw there was an inscription but he couldn't read it. "It's German", Wagner said "it says 'To my darling Hans who taught me the music of the heart. On our 30th Anniversary. Oct. 29, 1906. All my love, Sara'. My mother said that it used to play an old German song but when she was little she over-wound it and it broke. She said she cried all day. So her grandfather left it to her when he died. Just punishment I guess." Gray was speechless. "You know son, I have no children, only some cousins that I don't like very much. But this is supposed to come to you. Don't ask me why but I know it's true."

Annie was looking at it with wide eyes. "Could I see it, love?" Gray handed it to her and she turned it over in her hands looking at it from all angles. She pulled out the stem and pushed it back in and then she opened the watch. Crystalline music spread through the cold air. Wagner was amazed. "What the hell, the spring must have loosened up over time and when you pulled the stem it started it working again. But then why did they tell my father it couldn't be fixed? Or maybe it's just something about you, Annie darling. Is that it?" Annie smiled and hugged him.

"What is the name of that song." Gray asked. "Do you know? It seems familiar somehow."

"It's called 'the Linden Tree.' It's an old German folk song." Wagner said. "My mother used to sing it to me when I was young. My place is named for it- the Linden Tree Ranch."

"Thank you for the beautiful Christmas presents Hans. They are wonderful." Annie was smiling warmly.

Wagner smiled. "Ah sweet, there is something about you isn't there? So how did you know my name? I'm old but I think I would remember if I told you my Christian name. I haven't used it since my wife died. How did you know?"

She shook her head. "Come on, Wagner, you know women are intuitive. There was something in your face when you read the name on the inscription. I just knew it."

He climbed into his truck. "OK honey, if you say so. I'll see you all tomorrow."

After Wagner left, Annie hugged Gray. "Please don't let that business with Dewey spoil our Christmas, love. I still have to give you my presents." Gray shook himself to shed the negative feelings and smiled. "OK baby, but I'm afraid I'll need to deal with that guy sooner or later. And in things like that, sooner is usually better." Annie smiled. "Well, not now boy. Not on Christmas."

"Ok" he said grinning. "I have a present for you too; you know. Although I'm afraid Wagner's makes it look pretty feeble."

"Hans is a nice man and his gift is lovely, wonderful, certainly. But he's a very wealthy man and to him it was like giving away a balloon to a child."

"Maybe" Gray said, "If the balloon you gave the kid had been intended for someone you were once in love with... And if you kept it for years- and if it was made out of solid gold... And..."

"OK, OK. I still want your present more and I will love it forever." She sometimes got irritated by his insistence on precise definitions. He liked having the right labels on things. She thought the world should be more spontaneous. It conformed to her vision and fashioned itself out of chaos. And she wrote the labels herself.

He took out the package that he had carried in his pocket all day. It was wrapped in iridescent blue and silver and was somewhat the worse for wear. Inside she found a silver necklace.

"You see why Wagner's present bothered me?" Gray said. "I was so proud of this. A friend of mine made it. He's a silversmith and a jeweler."

She said "Oh Gray, it's beautiful! It must have cost you a fortune."

"It's a great blue heron. You know, for the Crossing." It was a turquoise pendant on a silver chain with the heron in flight embossed in silver across its surface. "It didn't cost that much. My friend owed me a little money and my father, my fine old grump of a father, lent me the rest. See, I told you that he liked you. If he hadn't he would have told me that he was broke."

Annie and Gray had had Thanksgiving dinner with his father and stepmother. "Of course that would be a lie. He's never broke. He never spends any money, so he can't be broke." Gray's father had been a lawyer for the city of Houston until he'd retired three years before.

Annie was all light and excitement. She uncovered a medium size package that had been under a blanket at the back of the tent. It was beautifully wrapped. "Now it's my turn." She smiled and brought the box over to the tree. The tree was about two feet high and strung with red and blue lights. It wasn't real but Annie had insisted that they have a Christmas tree. So there it stood on an ice chest, a plastic imitation of a tiny blue spruce direct from the great north woods- via China and Wal-Mart. The box contained a four track tape recorder that the band had been saving their money for. They needed one to make their demo records. It was a high quality brand that Gray knew was very expensive. After the 'you shouldn't haves' and thank you kisses, Gray said he needed to lock up. Annie smiled mischievously. "Don't get lost. I still have one more present for you."

When he returned to the tent he found Annie stretched out on top of the double sleeping bag wearing a wide grin, and a big red ribbon, and nothing else but goose bumps.

# 18

## HOSTILITIES

Annie hugged Gray and in her sweetest, sexiest voice said, "I love you baby. Don't worry. I'll be back in time for New Year's Eve." He kissed her goodbye and stepped back and closed the door to her car. He stood there watching her drive away to civilization, wanting desperately to follow her. He wouldn't see her for several days. She had to drive to Houston to celebrate a second Christmas with her family. She had hurt her parents' feelings by spending the holiday with him and now she had to be sweet and let them know that she still loved them. Across the intersection Dewey grimly watched the entire farewell scene from the shadows of his stand. Gray gave him the finger and turned back to his clapboard prison.

With Christmas behind him and Annie gone, Gray felt more trapped by the isolation than ever. This was not the way he wanted to spend his life- not even two weeks of his life. There must be more to living than just paying the stupid bills. "Damn Stanley anyway" he thought. Sure, he was trying to help but Gray would have found some way without this frigid solitary confinement. He was beginning to sink into a deep and unwieldy depression when Wagner drove up. He looked Gray up and down and poured them both a cup of Irish coffee.

"I take it your girl is gone?"

"Yeah, and it's pissing me off. I just hate being stuck here, you know? I should be going with her. I feel trapped. This is like being in the army or something."

"So when is she coming back?" The old man was grinning, which struck Gray as very uncalled for. He did not feel like laughing.

Gray grunted painfully. "New Year's Eve."

"Well son, that's not even a week away. I think you can make it. She'll come back before you know it. Surely you aren't worried about her changing her mind once she's out of reach of your mesmerizing presence? Or is it that you think her parents will convince her that she's made a mistake?"

"Oh hell Wagner, she's a rich kid. Her father's head of some big Houston bank. I'm an unemployed hippy musician. What business does she have with me?" The self-pity was gaining on Gray rapidly.

"OK my friend, I have a few things to say. And you need to listen." Wagner poured another slug of coffee. "First, and perhaps most importantly, this mood you're in isn't real. And I think you know it. This is just your ego dramatizing. It makes itself feel important by indulging in these bouts of emotions. It keeps the game exciting. But you know that nothing is going to come between you and Annie. I knew that the first time I saw you with her. It's Fate. You came here to be together. Her parents don't have a prayer." Gray rolled his eyes. "And anyway you aren't unemployed. You're an entrepreneur, a proud merchant in the great capitalist tradition. And you aren't some low life bum. You aren't even a poor boy. Your father was a Houston lawyer. How is that so different from a Houston banker? Hell son, they probably have lunch together. So you're a musician, so what? Whenever you get tired of that, quit. Go back and finish school if you need to. But I've heard your songs. You could make a living if you want to, if you just give up your need to struggle. And finally, Annie. You aren't imagining it. Annie is no ordinary girl. She is a truly special person. She has more personal power than anyone I know. I'm old. I've been around the World more times than I remember. I've lived in more countries than you can count. I've never met anyone like her before. She is different on some categorical level. I don't even know what it is, but it's real. Nobody, including you, is going to force her to do anything. It's not going to happen. And she loves you. End of sermon."

Wagner left early because the stand got really busy and it stayed that way right up to midnight. Everyone was getting in supplies for New Year's Eve. There are only three things that are absolutely essential for a good New Year's Eve: Skyrockets, champagne and a kiss. Gray smiled to himself. This year he had them all.

After the stand closed he sat in front of his tent drinking a beer and smiling at the night. Wagner's lecture had done him good. It shook him right out of his blues and back to reality. In a few days he'd be free and out of debt and with Annie. Life was good.

Suddenly the night went Technicolor with light. Two Chinese rockets exploded over his head. Blue and red stars melted into golden tears which trailed down into the shadows. The lights of the stand were off and the unexpected brightness momentarily blinded him. He ran around to the front side of the stand to see where the rockets came from, just in time to see another rise in fire from Dewey's stand across the street.

Gray started yelling. "Jesus, you moron, what the holy hell are you doing? Are you out of your mind? Do you want to blow us both up?"

A bottle rocket arced across the street in answer. It exploded against the large plywood door of the shop and went out in a red glow almost at his feet. The door was closed or he would already have been blown to hell. The next bottle rocket exploded just as it hit him squarely in the chest. While he was busy slapping at the sparks on his heavy woolen jacket, four Chinese rockets blew up in green and gold and red explosions against the stand, while blue fire erupted at his feet. He turned and ran behind the stand cursing his adversary while mortars exploded into color overhead. He wasn't sure what to do next. The problem was that Dewey had set all this up ahead of time, while Gray sat drinking beer. He had his whole counter covered with missiles aimed at Gray's stand. Eventually, even with the stand shut up, it would catch fire and the game would be over. Gray wasn't sure what it would be like when it blew but he didn't want to be crouching here to find out. He was tempted to fire back and blow his enemy's base up but he didn't want to kill anybody. And anyway, his stand would no doubt go up as well. Right now he realized the main danger was that Dewey would blow himself sky-high on his own.

He decided to try to negotiate with his lunatic adversary. "Dewey, just wait a minute man; you aren't making sense. You're going to kill yourself. You don't want to do that. We just need to talk it out."

For a moment the explosions stopped but the silence was pierced by Dewey's voice screaming. "Fuck you- you asshole!" And a new barrage began again immediately. Gray thought of all the cardboard boxes full of Black Cats and cherry bombs and mortars and Ground Blooming Flowers and chasers and bottle rockets and Chinese rockets stored under the display shelves and filling the portable shed behind the stand. He groaned. Strangely he didn't feel afraid. Somehow it almost felt like old drill. He decided that there was only one thing left to do. He had to jump Dewey, knock him out, tie him up, something. He moved to the opposite back corner of the stand and peered around it. He watched Dewey set off another round of rockets and then he ran straight at him across the intersection. Overhead the sky was alive with colors and the street was littered with rocket casings, many still on fire. It was about sixty feet to Dewey's corner and he made good time. He threw himself at the stand and slid across the counter to grab Dewey by the throat, landing on top of him in the narrow area behind it. He had no room to box with his opponent and he realized that Dewey's size put him at a disadvantage, but Gray was on top and there was no room to roll either. He slammed his fist into Dewey's temple and again into his nose. It was almost enough. But though he was stunned, the big man got his hands on Gray's jacket and pushed him away, twisting to get to his feet. They crashed through the stand's side door and rolled onto the ground outside with Dewey on top. Gray wondered if it was over, and then he noticed the blood welling on his enemy's forehead and into his closed eyes.

Trying to piece it together later, he decided that Dewey had hit a two by four strut when they crashed through the door and had knocked himself out. He rolled out from under his unconscious opponent and got to his feet, deciding to leave while he could. He didn't want to get himself killed. He had better things to do with his life right now. He'd go to the cops and let them deal with this maniac.

Moving across the intersection he saw that a fire had started in the pallets that served as a dry floor In front of the counter. He ran to put it out but it was too late. It was already spreading to the front of the stand. So he ran for the tent and grabbed the receipts, his guitar and the tape deck Annie had given him for Christmas and made for the old pickup truck. It seemed to take forever to start the damned thing but eventually it came to life. He forced himself to wait while it ran a little because he knew it would choke if he pushed it too quickly. He drove around the stand and out onto the highway. Then he thought of Dewey. He decided that he couldn't leave him to die and drove across to pick him up. But his attacker was already in his truck and driving away.

Gray headed toward the City at forty-five miles an hour, the old truck's top speed. As he drove he saw flashing lights coming towards him and pulled over to watch them pass. It was a fire truck. He made a wide u turn and followed it. Another approached from behind him. He pulled over to let it go by and then followed again at a respectful distance. He could see other flashing lights coming toward them from the other side of the stands. The Hector Volunteer Fire Department was not about to be shown up by the Norton Springs Volunteer Fire Department. There was a county sheriff's car and a highway patrol cruiser as well. While they were all still a quarter mile away from the intersection, his stand went up. It was unbelievable. Gray wondered who had called 911 because everything looked normal so far. But while that thought was still echoing through his mind everything started going off- rockets, mortars, chasers, missiles, fountains. It sounded like a battlefield in a heavy fire fight. Constant staccato explosions roared louder and louder. The noise alone was overwhelming. And then something flew into Dewey's stand and it started going up too. Wave after wave of black powder thunder rocked the night. At the base, the colors were an intense blue-violet which lightened to blue. The blue gave way to bright white light. The flames pulsated and leapt higher and higher at the base of a column of color that climbed half way up the sky. The left side of the column was a deep blood red which brightened to the right and became orange and then yellow. At the crown of the column it blossomed into star bursts of red and blue, green and gold. And it burned on and on for what seemed like a very long time but was actually perhaps only fifteen minutes. Then, at last, it began to subside.

On the local news that night there was an interview with the Norton Springs Volunteer Fire Department fire marshal.

"Well, there wasn't much we could do, really" he said, "except to keep it from spreading to the adjacent fields. But one thing we all agreed on- It was the prettiest fire any of us had ever seen."

# 19

## SARA'S NEWS

She woke in the morning to the girls' squabbling. She thought "Please no, not today." Her stomach was troubled and her head was hurting and she felt vaguely ill at ease with her world, as if the horizon had been skewed during the night. It almost seemed as if she had had too many glasses of wine, though she wasn't really sure what that felt like. It had only happened once, at her wedding. She had nearly fallen and Henry had picked her up in his great arms and carried her to their room as if she were weightless. He had helped her out of her gown then and had lovingly tried to wake her nascent passion. When it became obvious that she would rather sleep, he had kissed her and stroked her until she did. It was three days before they had their wedding night and his gentle attention never flagged. When they did make love at last she had been so in love with his kindness that she would have done anything he asked. It was a sweet night. Now though, she wondered if she was coming down with something.

After a slight struggle with Annie she had the girls dressed and downstairs to her mother's attention. Mama would feed them and talk to them in her brusque and loving way and watch over them until she came down. Her mother enjoyed the role of omi but didn't get carried away with it. She would help anyway she could, but she never tried to take over, and left Sara to make her own decisions about her children. She was a perfect grandmother, Sara thought, as she had been a perfect mother. And suddenly she knew why she was feeling bad. "Oh no! Oh dear God no!" And she was throwing up into the wash basin. "No!"

Since the midnight encounter with Hans, Sara had known no peace of mind. She felt guilty and embarrassed and sinful somehow, though she would have said she didn't believe in sin. Her parents were atheists and Freethinkers and had raised her without religion. Nonetheless, she felt somehow unclean, as if she had crossed some line that separated her from the "good people." At night in her bed she talked to Henry and told him how sorry she was that she had been unfaithful. Because that was how it felt- as if she had been unfaithful to her living husband; because he was still so alive to her. And now, if she was right about being pregnant, it was like some divine retribution from an angry god.

Her mother was worried about her. When she came downstairs she sat her down and gave her a cup of tea and toast with her blackberry jam.

"Darling, what is the matter? You are so pale. Are you ill?"

'No mama, just feeling a little strange today. I'm sure it's nothing."
"Well good. You just take it easy today. I'll watch Beth and Annie." She smiled kindly and patted her daughter's shoulder.

"By the way, you have a letter from Hans. Your father brought it home last night."

Sara went out to the porch with her tea and sat in her father's rocker reading her letter. It was dated the day after she and the girls left Mason.

*August 24, 1876*
*"Dearest Sara,*

*As I watched you and the children drive off with the Mitchells my heart was breaking. I have failed you all so badly, just as I fear I failed Henry. You all mean so much to me but there is no way that I can honor that love fully. Sara, you know that we can only hurt the memory of someone who means more to each of us than it is possible to say. There is more that comes between us that you don't know about, that I can never tell you or anyone but must always grow between us like a hedge of terrible thorns. There are already things between us that have caused you great pain and heartache. I cannot tell you how sorry I am for that. I can in no way make recompense for my failures and my mistakes. So I offer the only thing I can imagine that might weigh positively on the balance scales. I intend to hunt down and execute every man responsible for Henry's murder. I know I promised you that I would not seek vengeance. But in the year since Henry's death, not one of his murderers has been brought to answer for his crimes except for the man I killed myself. Henry's memory cries out to me for justice and finally I must answer. I hope I am right in believing that I have fully kept my promise to aid you in your endeavor to maintain a home for you and the children. We could not have tried harder to make it work. It seems that the Universe itself is at odds with our success in Mason.*

*I have sold all the stock. I got a fair price from Hager for the pigs. But I did less well with the cattle for Anderson's trail drive.*

*No doubt he'll get a good price in Kansas but he said Kansas is a long way off and I'm sure he is correct. Hager also bought the bay and the mustang, again for a decent price and he will keep Meg for you in case you want to send for her or reclaim her. I will enclose those monies in the form of a bank check drawn on the Fredericksburg bank. I know you still wish to make the ranch work and stubborn as you are I believe it could happen. I don't know why it's so important to you unless it's because of Henry, but believe me dear, he would not have wanted you to pursue this to your detriment, something I fear you may be in danger of doing.*

*I have made my deed over to you and it is filed with the county. There I have also filed my last will and testament, so that whatever I leave behind belongs to you as well.*

*There is talk of a reward for Random and his bunch so if I do well there it may be of some use. I expect no such outcome but one can hope. I must say it is my wish that you sell both places and use the money to start anew in some kinder spot, but you must follow the urging of your own heart- as now must I.*

*Please give my love to Beth and Annie and my best to your parents. Try if you can to forgive me. I only ever meant you good and no harm. Try to think well of me from time to time.*

*With love and best wishes,*

*sincerely,*

*Hans Miller*

With a cry Sara dropped the letter to the floor and began to weep in a terrible and hopeless despair.

Her mother raced to the porch and crouched in front of her. The girls watched wide-eyed from the door. "What is it darling? What's happened? Stop darling, stop. The girls are frightened." And on and on and on, patting her and shushing her and hugging her and begging her to say what was wrong, while

Sara desperately fought her anguish for control. At one point her mother picked up the letter from the floor and started to read it but Sara snatched it from her hands and crushed it to her bodice while she sobbed. Eventually the grief abated as her will regained control.

She began to speak. At first she mumbled as if she had lost control of her tongue. But slowly she began to make sense. "Hans is going to die." She said. "He wants to. He's going after the men who killed Henry and they're professional killers and there are too many of them and he will be killed."

"But why would he want to kill himself love?" Her mother struggled to understand. "He's a strong man, a good man darling. He has a strong code of honor and he wants justice for Henry. But I'm sure he'll be all right. He's also a very smart man. He won't get himself killed."

"No Mama, he'll die because he wants to die. He's wanted to die ever since he came back from Henry's murder. Oh, he worked hard. God knows how hard he worked. And he tried to help and tried to be sweet with the girls but always there was this shadow, this pain between him and everything else. He thinks he got Henry killed. I think it's because Henry followed his lead and died. So he blames himself. And there's something else; I don't know what it is. He's never told me, but it's there between us. I've felt it all year." And again she began weeping.

"Oh darling, you're in love with him. My poor baby... I'll be right back darling. I'll take the children in the kitchen and get them to finish breakfast. You drink your tea and collect yourself. When I come back we'll talk."

Sara knew there was no hope for her if Hans was killed. She knew it. She knew that he would marry her to give the baby a name. It was how he was, honorable and proud. He wouldn't want to, because he was not in love with her, but there was no question in her mind about how he would respond. But if he died before he heard... she would be disgraced. There would be no forgiveness from the people here. Good women did not... She began sobbing again. And the girls... what would happen to her beautiful daughters if she were shamed? She knew her father loved her, but even so he might turn her out. Despair settled on her heart with a chill as cold as death itself.

Suddenly she knew what she had to do. She had to tell Hans before he got himself killed. There was no other way, no other solution. After deciding that, it was only a matter of how to get word to him. But there was no easy answer to that either. It had taken his letter three weeks to find its way to her. Three weeks. He could already be dead by now. She began to cry again. No, she thought, he can't be dead. That would be the end of it. No, he must be alive and moving towards death and she must stop him. Then there was still a chance. And she must believe it to make it happen. She leapt to her feet and went racing up the stairs to pack her things.

# 20

## JUSTICE

**G**ray watched the deputy walk down the corridor wearing the blank expression of someone who'd rather be anywhere else, but doesn't want it to show. To Gray's surprise he stopped in front of his cell and pulled out his keys.

"All right O'Bryan, you are out of here."

He spoke dramatically, the way Gray's football coach used to speak in high school, as if he'd watched a movie scene over and over and then practiced his lines in front of a mirror.

Gray had been stuck in the "drunk tank" since they brought him in last night. It was the general holding cell for people who hadn't been charged or otherwise officially admitted to the system. He'd only had one cell mate, a college boy who was charged with possession of an ounce of cocaine. He was scared and arrogant and kept saying that his father was "gonna come down here and kick some ass." They'd taken him away about an hour ago.

There was a pay phone on the cell wall and Gray had called Arnie collect around seven-thirty, about as early as he could hope to wake him up. Arnie was his usual supportive self. "It's all over the news about the fire. The pictures keep playing on the tube. You really fouled it up this time."

That pissed Gray off. "Me? I didn't do anything except try not to get blown up. It was that jerk Dawson. The crazy bastard tried to kill me."

"Then why are you in jail? Why didn't they lock him up?"

"They did. He's right down the corridor from me. They took me in from the stand when I talked to the firemen about what had happened. The sheriff said they'd better lock me up until they'd 'sorted things out.' And then there was the pickup truck with no papers. They loved that. Then they brought Dewey in about three this morning. Locked him up down the hall. One of the jailers said they heard we were both being charged with arson."

"Well what the hell am I supposed to do about it?" Arnie blustered. "I don't have any money to bail you out. Do you want me to call your old man?

"No! Do not call my father! He'll give me shit about it forever. Find out how much my bail is and then try asking Alonzo. I think he might help me. Tell him I swear I'll pay him back. And Arnie... thank you for dealing with this for me, man."

"Look man, it's OK. We're partners..." Arnie paused. "You'd do the same for me. We'll get you out of here somehow."

But Gray had talked to Arnie at around seven-thirty. It was only ten-thirty now. That was way too quick for Arnie to have managed to get him out. He started worrying that his father had learned about it and had come to fix everything. So when he came out and found Wagner smiling at him he was as relieved as he was surprised.

"Now Gray" Wagner said with a broad grin, "didn't I tell you not to play with matches?"

Gray couldn't believe the old man had come to his rescue. "You bailed me out Wagner? You shouldn't have done that. How much was it? I swear I will pay you back every cent."

"My friend, I have the feeling you've rescued me a time or two. Anyway, let's not worry about that right now. We need to go have breakfast and talk about what happened and what we need to do about it. Gray O'Bryan, this is my lawyer, Mitchell Harris. Mitchell, this is the great songwriter and troublemaker that I was telling you about. Mitchell is a fan of Texas music, Gray. I gave him your CD and he really liked it."

Gray hadn't really noticed Wagner's companion. The attorney was a kind looking man in his mid-sixties, wearing sweat pants and a Willie Nelson t shirt. He was balding and overweight but he broadcast an air of confidence that made Gray trust him completely.

Wagner laughed. "Don't worry about the way he dresses son. He cleans up really well. Mitchell has been my lawyer since he escaped from law school. I promise you, he is extremely capable."

During breakfast at Denny's, Gray tried to explain what happened, and politely answer questions with his mouth full. The attorney said Dewey had called the police, claiming that Gray had assaulted him and left him for dead and set fire to his stand. The only witness was the passing motorist who'd seen the initial barrage and called it in on his cell phone, but he was too far away to tell what was really going on. The sheriff had picked up Dawson too.

"It seems your enemy is well-connected Gray," Harris said, "His attorney is on his way from Houston. He's a partner in one of the most important firms in the state. And he's a criminal lawyer, which, by the way, I'm not. If it gets to that stage, another man from my office will represent you."

Gray was suddenly nervous. "Are you saying that I could be charged with…" He paused, trying to think it through. "What, arson, assault, attempted murder? But I didn't do anything but try and keep that crazy fucker was blowing us both up."

"Now don't worry.' Mitchell Harris patted his shoulder. "I still have a lot of tricks to play before it comes to that. With any luck, it will never get that serious."

***

It was the day before New Year's Eve that Gray got the word from Mitchell Harris. He was sitting on his porch waiting for Annie to drive back in from Houston. A Mercedes sedan pulled into the yard with Harris driving and Wagner riding shotgun. Gray was worried until he saw Wagner's face.

"OK you outlaw" When he smiled Wagner's wrinkled old face was a study in joy. "You are free and clear. The fire marshal declared the fire an accident and the sheriff dropped all the charges against you, even the tickets for the truck."

"We told them that you were thinking about buying it so they called it a test drive and let it go." Harris was looking very pleased with himself.

Gray was puzzled. "What happened with Dewey?"

"Well, that was the deal that I made with his lawyer. Both sides would agree that nothing had happened, beyond the 'accident' I mean. No foul, no penalty. Like it never happened."

"But it did happen. The son of a bitch tried to kill me. Hell, he nearly did. You mean he just walks away?"

"Well Gray, there's something that you need to understand." Mitchell Harris looked very uncomfortable.
"This isn't about justice. It's about the law, and that's a very different thing. There were no witnesses to Dawson's attack. Right away that leaves it up in the air. If we went to trial it would be your word against his and who can say how that would work out? In front of a jury, a good lawyer and a good haircut can make a lot of difference. Would you really want to take a chance on spending a year or more in prison just to have a chance, just a chance, of bringing your enemy to justice? You'd be crazy if you did. Is this perfect? No it isn't perfect, but then so little is. I said that he was well-connected. Well he is. His father is a state senator. His mother is a leading

Republican fundraiser and big-time Houston socialite. Truth is, the only chance there was that this would ever go to trial was if his lot had wanted to hang you for it. But that couldn't happen." He smiled… "You're pretty well-connected yourself, you know."

Wagner patted Gray on the shoulder. "Don't worry about it son. The real wisdom is almost always in taking the path of least resistance. You may never see this fellow again. If you do he may be over it. If he starts trouble again, you'll have this history with him to fall back on. That will make it easier to get a hearing from the law. And if worse comes to worst, you won't be any worse off than you were before."

"There's more good news with this too." The lawyer was smiling again. "Because the fire marshal ruled the fire an accident, the fireworks company can't hold you liable for the stock they lost, which they initially wanted to do. You can pretty much tell them what you are going to pay, out of what you took in. They have insurance. It covers lost stock and even some of their lost revenue. I talked to Fredericks, the owner. He's reconciled himself to the loss."

"Which means Mitchell showed him how much better off he'd be if he just followed the path of least resistance… and avoided the court costs. And, unless I miss my guess, he made it obvious as pain. Didn't you counselor?" Wagner was grinning again. Gray tried to imagine that bony old face without his constant smile and couldn't.

He shook his head and turned to look the attorney in the eye. "Are you saying that I can keep all the money I took in?"

"Well no, not all of it. But because of the fire you can make your own accounting. The insurance will cover the rest."

Gray shook his head. "I know exactly what I took in before the place blew up. I did my sales report first thing every night. My percentage comes out to one thousand and eleven dollars ($1011). That's $6.02 an hour. Not exactly the get rich quick miracle that Stanley promised me but it's a thousand dollars I didn't have before. I'll settle up with Fredericks tomorrow."

"Whatever you like." The attorney said, "But a word of advice- I checked into Mr. Fredericks's reputation and he is rumored to be very difficult to collect from. I suggest you let me handle your final accounting."

"Thanks Mitchell, I really appreciate your help, but I'll do it. Mr. Fredericks is probably going to regret it now, but he never made it out to pick up the deposits like he was supposed to. I have all the money."

"Well then Brother Gray, at least give him the money that you owe him, not the whole amount. Then show him your paper work."

"Thanks. That much I will do. I also thought I'd give him a copy and ask if he wants me to submit a copy to the insurance company."

They were standing by the car laughing at a joke Mitchell Harris told about a cowboy, a lawyer, and a duck when Annie drove up waving. There were introductions and thank-yous and goodbyes. Gray and Annie accepted an invitation to dinner at Wagner's ranch for the next week, and then there was only Annie.

# 21

# THE AMBUSH

Hans waited for death in a cedar brake. He'd found a place where the road curved around a sheer limestone outcrop that offered passing riders no cover or shelter. The inside of the curve was a rocky slope heavily wooded with cedar and scrub oak. From his seat slightly above and at the radius point of the curve he had an uninterrupted view of about a hundred feet of road. The thick needles of his cover protected him from view from the road, yet left him room to pivot a hundred and eighty degrees. He had two rifles beside him and two pistols. He'd spent the first ten minutes clearing away the dry under- branches that might have been a problem. Now he just waited for his quarry to arrive.

His mind was wandering a lot as he crouched there in the heat with sweat and cedar needles trickling down his face and neck. While he waited he called up memories, of the woman, of Henry, of finding the ranch and chasing and being chased by Comanche, and worst of all, of the War. He remembered moments like this, almost exactly like this, in Virginia. Only he hadn't been alone. His company was spread out in some corn field beside some road, waiting for the Rebels to come by. Everyone was silent. Everything was still. You could hear flies droning, the dry whisper of the breeze in the leaves of the corn, a muffled curse. And then the Rebel cavalry came down the road and the roar of the first rifle volley drowned out everything for a moment. Then came the screams of men and horses, shouts of pain and surprise and anger, a few scattered shots of return fire and the drum of their horses' hooves as they rode from the trap to regroup. And all that remained were the pitiful, nerve-rending cries of the wounded, the dying, summed up in his abbreviated memory in one man's moans of "Jesus help me! Oh Jesus..."

He wondered at the human ability to live through such horror and remain sane. Some didn't of course. He remembered one of his company, a friend who'd been with him since New York, abruptly standing up and walking without a weapon toward enemy fire, his face smiling as he turned and walked through the veil of death. And there were others who simply left without warning, so that you never knew for certain whether they had deserted or died unseen. And did they remain sane, the survivors, simply because they kept going, kept living? Was he sane, crouching here all these years later, waiting to kill and die? No, he didn't think so, not in any way that mattered.

He was hunting a group of riders that he'd seen coming, from a spy point high up on the hill behind him, twelve men heading north at a steady gait. They matched the description he'd been given in Garnett's tavern by Hennessey, one of the Texican ranchers. According to the men gathered at the saloon, Cooper and Random and their bunch were headed north to kill Engels and burn him out. Engels was one of the leaders of the Germans in the area. He was a spokesman for

Mason's Freethinkers and had recently written an open letter to the governor. It was published in the papers. It asked him to send troops to end the Hoodoo War. He had said some things about the gunmen that had made Random angry and the gang was on their way to get even. Gray had ridden cross country to try and head them off, and most likely to die.

When the riders came into the curve he realized they were Germans, some of them friends of his, and he walked out to the road and hailed them. Twelve rifles leveled on his chest, and then Enders, one of his nearest neighbors, recognized him.

"For Christ's sake, Hans, what are you doing? You nearly got yourself shot."

Hans laughed. "None of you sons of bitches would have hit me anyway. Where are you going in such a hurry?"

"We're fed up with these dogs killing our friends" Enders answered. "They've killed Hoerster and Wohrle now. We've decided to run those gunmen to ground and hang the bunch. What are you doing out here alone?"

"The same thing I guess, only hanging never entered my mind." Hans wasn't smiling now.

The word went muttering through the ranks of the gathered horsemen. "Good thing we caught up with you then. At least you won't die alone." Enders was grinning.

Someone down the line said- "Bad luck! Let's not speak of dying."

Hans said loudly, "Luck's got nothing to do with it. If you go to kill, you go to die. And make no mistake, murder is murder and dying is dying- alone or with friends." Then he explained about Random and their enemies' planned attack on Andreas Engels's homestead. "I hoped to get ahead of them and ambush them here. I thought if I did it could help Andreas and his family. At least the sounds of the rifles might make them more aware, and if I was too late, then I'd make the bastards pay my toll on their way back. I haven't heard any gunfire, so I think I beat them here. I suggest we send a lookout up the hill to watch the road, and then set the same trap, only better."

A number of these men had fought in the War on one side or the other. Some fled the area to join the North. Some stayed and were conscripted by the South and went along rather than go to prison. Those who stayed behind were hard-pressed by the Comanche while the armies were away at war. Very few of them were new to battles and death. They went about the tasks of setting their trap quickly and quietly.

When the lookout signaled riders coming they were ready.

It was just over one hundred and eleven feet from the point that the outlaws rode into the kill zone until they rode out at the other end. Fourteen men rode into the trap moving at a canter with Cooper at their head. "Kill the ones before you" was the final instruction. The ambushers were thirteen, the riders fourteen. Hans knew the scene from his nightmares. The roar of the volley, the screams of men and horses, from his place at the far end he could see it all. He watched the riders fall from their saddles with their blood spraying from their wounds. He heard the prayers and groans of their dying. His first bullet hit Cooper below his left arm, piercing his heart from the side. Cooper pulled back on his reigns automatically and his horse reared. He toppled forward across his saddle and fell to the ground as the horse bolted from beneath him. Before he finished falling, Hans had fired another round into his back. Then he turned his attention to a rider still on his horse who was charging past him heading out of the trap. He didn't have time to get another shot off but someone down the line hit the man from behind. He fell forward on his horse's neck but held on and rode out of view still in the saddle.

Ten bodies lay bleeding in the dirt below the posse. Four escaped. Besides the wounded rider at Hans's end, three had made it out of the bottom of the trap. Two were bringing up the rear and weren't really in it to begin with. The third had a great, fast horse, a big black, and had dropped down on his neck and turned him very fast and disappeared. On his way out he'd gotten off three shots from his pistol. Two of them hit Karl Unger and killed him instantly. Unger was the son of one of the Adelsverein leaders, the original German immigrant wave in the 1840's. He had a young wife and a new son. He was nineteen. He was the posse's only casualty. Hans knew from the description of the horse that Random had escaped him unhurt. His job wasn't finished but he'd made a start. He felt no joy in it. If anything, the empty place inside him grew darker.

Five members of the group grabbed their horses and rode out in pursuit of the escapees. Rob Enders rode to tell Andreas Engels what had happened, in case Random still planned to attack his home. The rest gathered up the outlaw's horses and began tying bodies over their saddles for transport back to town. The ground here was rocky and pools of blood stood in places where the fallen had lain. As Hans left to join the pursuit he looked back at the trap. There were boot prints in blood all over the killing zone and vultures circled on the pale blue sky.

# 22

# THE PINTA TRAIL

"Don't do this darling! You'll kill yourself and your child! Wait until your father comes home, please darling! Wait! Wait!"

Her mother's voice still rang in Sara's head as she watched the stars blink into view above the wide valley she skirted. She was following the Pinta Trail but she rode the ridge above it against a line of cedars so that she would not be discovered by her father and his search party. She had watched them ride past below her, earlier, while she hid in an oak grove. There were five men riding hard, her father in the lead. She hadn't seen them since, but she wasn't taking chances. As full dark settled on the ridge, she dismounted and led her horse back into the trees, working her way ever deeper into a cedar thicket, until she felt that even in daylight she would be out of sight. There she made her bower, as harsh as any could be.

Charlemagne nickered as she stroked his nose. He was her father's best horse, his favorite, and she'd taken him from the stables knowing that it wasn't right. But he was big and fast and strong, and very sweet, the perfect horse for a long and dangerous journey. He was also brave and unafraid of gunfire, which could be important at some point. She would need the best horse she could get if she were to find Hans. And she had to find him. Her weakness earlier in the day embarrassed her. But once she began her search she allowed none of it. Perhaps other women would be afraid, hiding in a cedar break in the dark. She would allow no fear to weaken her resolve. She told herself that to win this race she must endure whatever came. If she must die, she would die, but she would die with her eyes open and her will determined. Nothing else would serve her cause.

She clutched the pistol that Henry had given her the day they came home to Mason and taught her to use over the course of six months. It was a .44 Colt and big for her hand, but he said she could master it and she had. She also could fire a Winchester rifle as well as most men. He told her that her spirit would see her through anything. She hoped he was right.

The Pinta Trail was the teamsters' trail used by the freight wagons that brought the stuff of civilization to the settlements of Texas. It went from New Braunfels in the east and San Antonio in the south to meet in Boerne. From there it went almost straight north to the trading post at Luckenbach, where it turned west to Fredericksburg and Mason and out to Menard at the edge of the Great Plains. It followed a route that had been here forever, because it was the path of least resistance through the high limestone bones of the Texas Hill Country. It was a series of the shortest possible paths- from this low water crossing to that lowest pass through the hills, stretching all the way from Mexico to the Great Plains. The herd animals, the buffalo and the deer and the antelope, and in ages past, the mammoth and the mastodon, had first marked it, always following their hunger. And the predators followed theirs as well, including Man, the most successful of them all. For thousands of years human tribes pursued the herds. No doubt they took the same shortcuts that Sara now followed. It was only the more modern members of those tribes that concerned her now though, the Europeans and the Comanche.

She knew that a woman was at risk simply from being a woman. To counter that threat she had cut her long and beautiful hair at the hairline above her shoulders. She had blanched at the idea, but she knew that it was necessary. Then she found her little brother's clothes that her mother had kept after his death three years ago. They were in his room in his dresser as if he might put them on again tomorrow. He had died of a fever the doctor couldn't identify and her girls were living in the room he left empty. But her mother would not let Sara move his clothes to make room for theirs and so they shared her dresser. The clothes were a little big for her but he had only been sixteen when he died and she could make do. His jacket and shirt were fine and she cinched up her belt to keep her pants on. She pulled his hat down low to cover her bright hair. It would do, she felt, at a distance, and she was counting on Charlemagne for that.

When dawn arrived she was already awake and peering down onto the trail from the cedars. Ahead of her only a mile or so was the break in the hills that the creek ran through. A sheer limestone cliff rose up on both sides of the water course, making the pass unavoidable. It was her only real concern. If her father or his friends were waiting there she could be pinned in and forced to return to New Braunfels. Perhaps there was a way over the hills behind her somewhere but she didn't want to waste her time or her horse searching for it. But to her relief when she neared the pass she saw no one waiting. If they watched on the other side she felt certain she and Charlemagne could outrun them. She could ride as well as anyone and better than most. But they weren't there. There was only another valley and more forest and prairie and she settled in for the long ride.

Mason was over a hundred and twenty miles away, many days ride for a strong man on a good horse, a very long week for a single pregnant woman. She put her hands on her stomach a moment and spoke to her child- "Listen my darling, my own. Be strong; be well. You are needed and wanted here. Already I love you with my whole heart. You must stay with me and keep me company. I feel very much alone. Do not fail and wither. Thrive and grow strong. I promise you we will live a fine life together you and I, full of learning and love and wonder. Stay with me; only stay with me." She searched for a name to call her child and suddenly she knew beyond doubt that she carried a girl. She could see her face and knew her name. "Clara... I love you pretty Clara." And she smiled as she rode into her future.

# 23

# NEW YEAR'S EVE

**"I**f every daydream came true as well as this one has," Gray said, "I'd do nothing but daydream from now on." He was sitting on the steps at Lorien and holding Annie's hand and sipping champagne while Hank and his bartender and busboys were lighting Chinese rockets in the parking lot. The sky was alive with brilliant color. The strains of *Auld Lang Syne* were spilling down the street from the houses in the neighborhood across the boulevard from the restaurant. There was more than one rendition playing, maybe several. If they had been loud it would have been irritating, but far away and faint, they seemed almost magical, even a drunken group chorale. Trust Texas, Gray thought, to offer up a New Year's Eve with temperatures in the sixties and all the doors open. Last year his pipes had frozen. Last week on Christmas Day he and Annie and Wagner had frozen. You just never knew.

It was five minutes after twelve midnight. He'd had his New Year's kiss from Annie that promised him the most interesting year ever. Beth sat on his other side laughing at her husband and everyone was toasting the old year and the New Year and friends and love and skyrockets and anything else they could think of worth toasting. It was probably because Wagner brought a case of Veuve Clicquot champagne to the Lorien company pot luck as his contribution. Wagner was sitting at a table on the porch behind them sharing a bottle with Hank's parents and the elders appeared to be having a good time. The entire company was in great good spirits. The fireworks crew was breaking the law but when the law showed up, Wagner spoke to the policeman and accepted the ticket. Gray wondered what it would feel like to never have to worry about money. He thought he could handle it.

Something Hank had said to Beth had sparked a feminist battle with the women, Beth and Annie and the other waitresses. They declared that they would handle the grand finale to prove that men were no more adept with explosives than women. Annie thought it was funny. She knew that she was equal to anyone and she didn't have to prove it, but Beth was taking it seriously. She was a firm advocate of a woman's ability to do anything as well as a man. She was an elegant and beautiful woman who looked like she should be the spoiled wife of some wealthy British noble or minor princeling from the south of France. Probably, she could have been if she had wanted to be. Except that she was fierce, and strong, and driven. Nothing made her angrier than women accepting the role of helpless victim. She was actually the dominant force in the business. Hank created the culinary masterpieces and ran the kitchen but she did everything else. She was very good at it and her staff loved her. Lorien was doing better every year and she was already talking about opening other restaurants and merchandising products from their kitchen.

The men had exhausted their supply of incendiaries and the women went down to the blast zone. Their finale would have been impressive even in a much grander setting. The rockets went up in four stages, each more elaborate and in a different color than the one before. There were four of them and, at the same time, two multi-shot mortars were going off. It was a truly a great finale.

"Sorry guys," Gray yelled "the women win by a landslide."

Hank's mother was yelling. "Way to go ladies! Teach that boy of mine some respect!"

Hank said "Hey, that wasn't a fair contest. Where did you get professional fireworks from anyway? We just went to the stand for ours."

Beth rose to the challenge. "It doesn't matter. There were no rules about the source. They were just fireworks like yours. They weren't made by the elves or anything."

Gray was watching Annie and saw an exchange of smiles take place between her and Wagner on the porch and thought maybe he knew who the elf was.

A few minutes later the party began shutting down. Everyone joined in to clean up the fireworks litter in the parking lot, and collect their dishes and clear tables and sweep. It was the same routine as most nights but more people were present so it took less time. On New Year's Day, Lorien was having a party for the public with free black-eyed peas and champagne. It wasn't Veuve Clicquot but it would be fun.

Gray's Liberators were playing. Tomorrow's party kept the workers from drinking too much tonight. Nobody wanted to work with a hangover, especially with their bosses watching.

The cops showed up again but saw the party was over and didn't stop. They just cruised by slowly. Annie waved to them and they waved back smiling.

Annie and Gray were staying at her apartment, which was only a couple of miles away. They were pleasantly happy from the champagne, Gray a little more so, but Annie was driving so he was OK. When they went in to the apartment he realized that something was wrong. It took them a moment to see the wind blowing the window curtains and the sparkle of glass spread across the living room floor. And in the center of the room, a brick lay on the carpet, no note, nothing else. There was just a brick and a window's worth of broken glass. It was an anonymous Happy New Year's message. They didn't have to discuss it. They both knew who the sender was. Annie was very upset. They swept up the worst of it. Tomorrow they would vacuum. Gray made a temporary fix with a cardboard box and they went to bed.

Annie put her head on his chest. She was shaking. "Hey sweetheart, it's all right." Gray tried to calm her. "Don't be frightened. It will be OK. Tomorrow we'll call the police and report it."

"Frightened?" She sat straight up. "I'm not frightened. I'm furious! I want that insignificant pipsqueak's head. How dare he? I mean, how dare he attack us? I want to just obliterate him so that he disappears completely. It frustrates me that I can't. But I promise you. He will regret it just the same!"

## Intermezzo II

*Her dreams are lightning and thunder. The darkness crackles with long, unbearably bright strands of fire. She calls her power. She wants to hold it in her hands. In her dreams she knows the center of the light where all power comes from. At her prompting mountains collapse into gravel, into sand. She delivers them to the sea. At her command the winds uproot forests and scatter them far away. Her floods drown cities. Her songs are war songs and anthems. Anger and death grow in her. She will not be insulted. She will not be attacked. Those blasphemies will be severely punished.*

*But something is wrong. Her power is thwarted. Her anger is ineffective. Her songs sound strangely thin, and weak. Then she remembers. She is not herself. She is in masquerade as a mortal. She has placed her power temporarily beyond her own reach. For a moment she regrets the whole foolish notion. Then she remembers love... and she smiles.*

# 24

## DEWEY'S SHADOW

Dewey sat at the window of Slomo's apartment watching Annie's place across the street. He couldn't see much there anymore, not since he'd started getting their attention. Now they were careful at night to keep everything covered up. He realized that Annie could make things difficult for him but he didn't know how bad it would get. He was just so pissed off that he didn't care. After the thing on New Year's, his father had called and told him to come home immediately or he would stop his allowance. And that wasn't the worst part. His mother had called him crying and had kept it up the whole time they talked. She wanted him to come home too, but mostly she wanted him to "be a good boy." She said it over and over again. She'd been saying it over and over again as long as he could remember. She told him she loved him over and over too, but he didn't believe any of it. They only adopted him because it would look good with their social set. His mother was a terrible social climber. She'd come from a poor family and married a construction worker and she had driven him constantly to do better, be more. And it had worked. He owned a big construction company and they were well-regarded in Houston society. And now because of her drive, his father was a state senator, a big, nice-looking, congenial guy and the perfect self-made man, self-made for politics. They were talking about lieutenant governor soon.

He turned the binoculars to the upstairs right apartment that the two dance majors shared. He had first found this place because of them. He had been sitting at the bar one night at the Fancy Tan. The two dancers had come in tight skirts that barely covered the legal tender. They were so hot he had to say something, so he told the guy sitting next to him at the bar that it should be against the law.

Slomo, short for Slomovich or something, was this great big guy with mean eyes and a bad temper who he'd seen there a few times before. He'd been a student on a football scholarship but he'd gotten in trouble for date rape and lost his shot. They'd dropped the charges but the coach dropped him as well.

He wasn't very bright, a few stops short of the terminal, some guy told Dewey once, and he made his living working heavy construction and collecting for bookies and loan sharks. He was always chewing gum and he always chewed his gum like he had a grudge against it. Slomo told him that he lived across the street from the dancers and said the view could be "extremely interesting" at times.

It was pretty interesting right now, he thought. There was only one girl home but she was getting ready to go out. It was twilight and the bright bathroom lights revealed everything. He watched her undress and step into the tub to shower. Through the high-powered binoculars he could see the dimples on her nipples and count the hairs between her legs, until the shower curtain closed. Then he had to wait until she got out and dried herself and then sat on the edge of the tub to apply her lotions and powders. By the time she put her bra on he was shaking. Damn it!

He hadn't really paid attention to Slomo's talk until he started talking about this other fine-looking girl who played piano all the time. Dewey asked him where he lived and when he told him Barrio Pescal, he realized that the big man had been talking about Annie. He bought the drinks and invited himself over for a look. It was the garret apartment across the street from Annie's fourplex. With the binoculars you could see everything in all the front rooms of her apartment building. Slomo was behind in the rent even though it was really cheap. Dewey had offered to pay half the rent if he could hang out there to "follow the ladies from time to time." Slomo jumped at the chance. Then after the fireworks thing he'd decided that he should lay low for a while and he'd moved in. It had an outside entrance in back and very little traffic so it worked well. Of course, without his allowance the arrangement would have to stop. He'd need to find another place to crash.

Suddenly he realized that the lights were on in Annie's apartment. Annie. Annie broke his heart. Lots of girls said they liked him and told him how cute and funny he was. But with most of them he knew that they were lying. They just wanted a rich husband and they knew his family was wealthy. He knew he was nothing. He'd known it all his life. But with Annie it was different. She told him he was cute and he believed her. She laughed at his jokes and he laughed along. He had never been as happy as he was with her. He knew he didn't deserve her. Hell, nobody deserved her. She was perfect, amazingly beautiful and talented and passionate. Making love to her was like nothing he had ever known before. And so he blew it. He couldn't help it. He needed her to be his. He had to try and make it permanent. And when she said no, he couldn't let it go. He couldn't be calm and wait. And he lost her. He hated himself for it and he hated her. But, most of all, he hated that fucking musician, that asshole.

Every time he saw them together coming out or going in they were laughing and having a good time- every time. Twice through the window he had watched them kiss. He had waited until the middle of the night and then he'd gone down and slashed the tires on Annie's car. Then yesterday he watched them making love in Annie's living room where she and Dewey had made love last year. He had driven out to the asshole's place early this morning and shot out all his front windows with his deer rifle. He loved that rifle. His father had given it to him for his thirteenth birthday when he'd taken him deer hunting. He taught Dewey to shoot and helped him get his first deer. It wasn't much of a trophy but his father acted like it was and hung the rack on the wall in his office. It was the only time he'd taken Dewey anywhere. His father gave him his .44 too, when he left home. "Just in case" he said, but he didn't say in case of what. Still, he was glad he had it now. It made him feel stronger, more in control. For years he had never taken it out of its case but he carried it everywhere now. It had a holster that he wore under his shirt behind his back.

If her lights were on she must have parked off the alley in the back and gone inside through the back door. That meant that she was hiding from him. Strangely, it gave him a sense of connection to her, as if her fear of him was an emotional bond.

And he guessed it was. Whatever, he just couldn't stand not being in her life, seeing her laugh, holding her.

He was interrupted from his longing by the door of the apartment opening. Slomo came in, walking stooped over to keep from hitting his head on the rafters of the attic room. He was smiling happily. He liked the arrangement he had with Dewey and Dewey took pains to keep it that way. He called the big moron "partner" and tried to make him feel like his best friend and it was working. He was easily led, as long as Dewey made him feel important.

"Getting' an eyeful man?"

"Shoot partner, you missed it. Hmm, hmmn, hmmn…"

"What man, what did I miss? Did they finally take a shower together? Man I been waiting for that."

"Nah, it wasn't that good. It was just the brunette; but buddy, I got to see it all."

"Damn it!" The big man was more frustrated than Dewey was by the frequent displays. Dewey could afford to cool off down on Peckham Street for fifty bucks but Slomo was too broke for that kind of relief. Suddenly a plan emerged full-blown in Dewey's head.

"You know, I sure would like to have some of that" he said in his friendliest voice. Slomo muttered his agreement. "But that's not going to happen. Those girls are so stuck up that they'd never have anything to do with a couple of regular guys like us. Sometimes I wish it was like in the old days, like the

Cossacks or the Comanches. Just come riding down out of the hills and grab you one. That would be so cool."

Slomo was all ears now. He laughed. "I'd get both of them, one under each arm." He sounded like a kid all of a sudden, playing cowboys and Indians.

"Yeah those were the days" Dewey went on. "I mean it's not like it hurts them. Those two probably fuck some new guy every night, at least every week. What would one more hurt?"

"I know" the thug said smiling. "I thought that a lot. I mean, what's the big deal, right?"

"Really. I'll bet," Dewey said, "a guy could still do that if he had the balls for it. You know, scoop some girl up and carry her off."

"Sure" Slomo said, "If he didn't mind going to prison."

"Hey, people get away with it all the time. Not long ago I read where some guy in Virginia kept this girl in his basement for three years. He only got caught because a neighbor had a gas leak and when the crew was looking for it, the gas company guys knocked on the basement door and the bitch started yelling. Just bad luck for him. You know how many beautiful women just disappear every year? Where do you think they are?"

"Yeah, I guess" the big man said, "but I wouldn't want to keep them prisoners forever. You know?"

"Well sure, but you wouldn't have to. As long as you were careful not to let her see where you took her and you kept her blindfolded so she couldn't see your face, you could drive around for a while and then let her out way out in the country somewhere. The law could never trace you."

"But you'd have to have some place to keep her where she wouldn't get found by the gas company." Slomo was thinking now.

"Well," Dewey said, "as if he were just thinking of it, "how about our hideout?" The two had found a basement room in the old cotton gin. It had probably been a tool room or some mechanic's office. They'd been stalking Annie and the musician across the river. Dewey had started it as a kind of game, bringing Slomo in because nobody would connect him to the situation with Annie. Then he made Slomo feel like it was a great game for a couple of good buddies, good ten year old buddies Dewey thought. But it worked to bring Slomo on line as his perfect shadow and henchman. The relationship would work as long as Dewey's money held out and he could pay the rent and buy the drinks. But even without his allowance he'd had nearly ten thousand dollars in the bank. And he got five grand for his truck and he only paid five hundred for the piece-of-crap car he bought. He had it all in hundred dollar bills and he had it stashed where no one would find it. He always kept a thousand with him. It had felt great to hold all that money in his hand at one time, all those beautiful one hundred dollar bills and change... He could get used to that. His father had cancelled his credit cards but the cash was more fun anyway.

"How would you get one do you think?" he asked the dummy. "I mean, if you were going to scoop one up?" Slomo's eyes were peering through the binoculars at the windows on the street. He didn't answer. "I'd park a van, like yours, that didn't have any windows except in front, around back in their alley. I'd park between the building and their car and when they went to get in I'd be sitting in the open cargo door and drag them in. If they struggled I'd hit them in the side of the head and quiet them down and then I'd pull them in and close the door. Nobody would see a thing. Tie them up and drive away, simple as you please. Same way you told me you do it when you're collecting."

Slomo put down the binoculars and turned to Dewey. "Do you really think you could do it? And get away with it?" His eyes were intense, riveted on Dewey's face.

"Hell, I know we could if we worked together. I'd check out the cars and see what was back there. They don't always park back there, you know? And sometimes boyfriends and friends might come over. Then when it all looked right, you could drive your van over there and I'd watch through the binoculars and when one of them got ready and turned out the lights and left, you could be parked alongside them and scoop them up. Cool!"

"But how would we know it's the dancers?"

"It doesn't need to be the dancers." Dewey answered, "If it is fine, but there are only four women in that place. One apartment is empty. There's the two dancers, the piano player and the redhead. They're all gorgeous, so who cares which one you bring home?" He knew which one it was going to be, but the muscle didn't need to know anything about Annie. He wasn't sure how he'd keep Slomo from going at her, but he'd figure it out.

Slomo smiled in anticipation. "So we're really going to do it, right? We really are? We aren't just talking?"

"Yeah partner, we really are. In the meantime, how'd you like to help me teach an acquaintance of mine a lesson?"

"Sure, I guess. Some guy giving you trouble Dewey?"

"Yeah man. He stole my girl friend, and that would be OK, but he treats her like shit and beats her up and stuff. He's a real asshole. But he's a boxer and when I tried to stop him he nearly broke my jaw. I'd like to even the score and teach him not to pick on girls, especially my girl."

"Damn. Sure man. We'll teach him not to mistreat women."

"Great. Thanks. Let's go. We can take my car." Dewey was practically laughing. He thought, "This will be a piece of cake. This is going to be fun."

## 25

## BAD DREAMS

New Year's Day morning, Gray called the police while Annie went to work on ending the Dewey problem. Gray could not have imagined the level of anger and intensity that she showed. She called her parents and told them what had happened and insisted they call Dewey's parents to put pressure on him. Her father had been instrumental in Dewey's father's election to the state senate. Annie's mother was a major mover in Houston society and had been helpful in getting Dewey's mother in with her crowd. Annie's parents agreed to do as she asked, but they both insisted that she come home immediately. When she refused, her father wanted to send her a bodyguard. The offer made Gray see Dewey's affront in a new light.

The cops were not very comforting. They seemed to think it was all "college kid shenanigans" as the older one put it. The younger of the two, who said he'd just graduated in criminal justice two years before, was more attentive, especially after they told him about Dewey. Gray told them about the fireworks stand and the young cop nodded. "I remember that story. I was at county delivering a couple stoners when they brought him in. He was acting like a real fool, talking about how they would all be sorry they messed with him, that he had connections, blah, blah… sorry fool."

As the police were leaving, the younger one lagged behind and told them that he'd check and see what Dewey had been up to that night and let them know how it went. He advised them to be careful and told Annie to be cautious about traveling alone and keeping her door locked at home. "Just pay attention" he said. "You'll be all right."

Gray listened to her complaints about her father's overprotectiveness at length after she got off the phone with them. "Annie darling, why don't you let your father send you a bodyguard? I think Dewey is dangerous."

Annie scoffed. "He's not dangerous. He's an idiot but he's not dangerous. He's just looking for attention. He's a spoiled rich kid throwing a temper tantrum because I rejected him. Ignore him and he'll go away."

Gray was not convinced. "You know, he really tried to kill me at the fireworks stand, and he was willing to blow himself up to do it. That's a lot more than a temper tantrum."

Annie shook her head. "He wasn't trying to kill you. He's an emotional child and he responds like a child. He thinks nothing through; he does the first thing he thinks of without considering the consequences. He's just stupid. And I'm not going to let him make me afraid and let my father, bless him, stick a spy in the middle of my freedom." She came over and put her arms around his waist. With her head on his chest she said, "We are fine darling. He's not dangerous, just annoying."

Gray wanted to believe her but the fireworks stand and the memory of Dewey's hate-filled face kept getting in his way. He was convinced that Dewey was insane, and dangerously so. At times he thought that Annie's supreme self-confidence blinded her to the real world around her. It was as if she thought nothing bad could possibly happen to her, even after reading the morning paper every day with its catalogue of horrors.

But the afternoon party at Lorien was about to start. They had called in telling Beth about what happened and that they were going to be a little late because of the police. Gray had called Arnie and told him to start without him but not to panic. He was on his way. Even Arnie seemed understanding.

New Years. It had started out so strong but already seemed to be going out of control.

The party for the public only lasted until five. There was some talk of starting up again where New Year's Eve left off but it didn't get much support. Most of the crew and the band had done their systems enough damage to last awhile. The band packed up and left and Gray helped clean up the restaurant to get Annie away faster. Then they were home, while the twilight splashed shadows down the quiet street to the evening chatter of the birds preparing for darkness.

He started to reopen the conversation about her safety but she lifted her head to kiss him and he forgot about Dewey. They made love in the living room while Sunday slipped away into bliss and long bare limbs perfect breasts soft warm mouths lips and tongues and stroking touching grasping gasping breathlessness and all moving in slow motion in a world as yielding and encompassing as the sea. Full dark was settling on the trees when they looked around again. The day had disappeared into streetlights blinking on to the rhythm of Annie's beating heart.

The next morning Annie woke him with a kiss. She was smiling and looking wonderful. Once again, for the ten thousandth time, he blessed his good fortune. She hadn't even showered or gotten ready for the day and she was already beautiful anyway.

"Hey babe, good morning. I'm off to the store to buy coffee. Sorry to wake you but I didn't want you to worry if you woke up when I was gone."

"Don't get lost" he said through a yawn, as he pulled the sheet up over his head. He teetered on the edge of sleep as Annie pulled the door shut behind her. He had almost caught up to his dream when the front door opened again and Annie came back in shrieking.

"Damn him! I am going to kill him! The son of a bitch slashed my tires. Two of them, the two on the street side."

"Wait a minute…" Gray struggled to surface again into consciousness. "Are you sure that they aren't just flat? Maybe we ran over something…"

"Of course I'm sure! There are two four inch cuts in the sidewalls. The son of a bitch slashed them!"

It was after twelve before the cops left and one-thirty before the crew from Goodyear finished changing the tires. The cops were the same ones who'd shown up about the brick through the window the day before. This time they were a lot more concerned. They took down all the information Annie could provide about her ex but the younger one informed them that he had checked and that Dewey was no longer living at his old address and had left no forwarding address. He'd told his former landlord that he'd sold his red truck for a lot less than it was worth and was going on an extended vacation. Then he'd seemingly disappeared.

Louise, Annie's neighbor from across the hall, loaned them enough coffee for a pot and Gray made mac and cheese in a box for breakfast or lunch, whichever it was. Louise was a beautiful and angelic grad student with a cloud of curly red hair for a halo. She was working on her masters in theater and everyone loved her. Twice Annie had made Gray go to see her productions. The second time didn't require as much pressure. Louise played the lead and directed it. It was wonderful. She was wonderful. In the few months since Annie had moved in they'd become great friends.

There were two dance majors in the flat above Louise. Susan focused on modern dance, though she bridled at the term modern. She said "How can they call it modern when it goes back to WWI? They should change it to Post Modern or something more imaginative." Sue thought anything that happened before she was born was ancient. Catherine, her roommate had no such problem. Her focus was ballet. Annie had taken Gray to three dance recitals, his first ever. He was surprised to find he liked both the classical ballet and the free form. All that grace in motion made the music visual, he told Annie. She gave him her concerned motherly smile that said something like: "I wonder if he'll ever learn to talk."

Sometimes the entire building would have parties. Once, Gray got a special dispensation from Alonzo and they had one at the Crossing. Alonzo and his wife even made an appearance and ate a hamburger and shared a beer. When they left early pleading age, the kids all asked them to stay. Gray called the apartment building the Barrio Pescal Center for the Arts. All three of Annie's neighbors had long standing boyfriends or fiancés and it was a ready-made social club. Usually when they partied the band would come too and bring dates. Two of the guys had built a fire pit in the back yard and they would sit around some weekends and play guitars and sing. All in all, it had been a perfect fall semester and more fun than Gray had ever had when he was in school. But this thing with Dewey was threatening the whole scene.

Two days after the tires were slashed, Gray decided that it was time to head out to Blue Heron Crossing and listen to the river. He dropped Annie off at Lorien and drove out to Morning Star feeling like he was escaping from a bad dream. When he got to the Crossing he realized there was no escaping this dream until he resolved it. The moment he opened the door he felt like he was falling off a cliff. Every window on the front of the house was scattered across the floor in glittering fragments. His plates and dishes, the pictures on the opposite wall, everything, was shot to hell. There were bullet holes in the walls. One bullet had gone through a hollow door and knocked out a window in his bedroom. The rest were presumably buried in the books in the bookcases or in the stucco walls. It was an enormous amount of damage. Now he was certain that he'd been right. He looked out the windows and saw nothing threatening. He was amazed that he wasn't afraid. He thought he should be, but all he felt was vigilant. Once again he had to deal with the police. This time it was the county sheriff's department. As soon as he had determined that Gray wasn't a hippie drug lord and that this wasn't some drug deal gone bad, the deputy became clearly worried about him and took down all his information and his suspicions about Dewey. He said he thought the shots had come from the old gin across the river. He said he would check over there for shell casings and clues. And he promised he would work on finding Dewey, but he didn't want to get Gray's hopes up, saying Dewey could be hard to find. As he left he promised to call with regular updates.

When he was gone, Gray measured up the windows and went to Ace Hardware to get new glass. By the time he had the place sealed against the weather, it was nearly time to pick Annie up from work. He didn't even have time to finish cleaning up. He drove to her restaurant and parked out in the back parking lot to wait where he always did. He was sitting in the car dozing when suddenly the door opened and he was dragged out of the seat by some massive force. A huge man was throwing him up against the side of the car and driving a jack hammer into his solar plexus. It took him a long time before he could suck wind again, meanwhile the great fists were drilling into him. Then the big man yanked him off the car and pinned his arms behind him. And there in front of him was Dewey, laughing and punching him in the face.

"I told you we weren't finished asshole. Well, here, I, am!" And with each word he hit him again. Gray felt the World moving away and leaving him behind in the Void.

Suddenly there was a lot of noise and movement and he was released to fall to the pavement. Arms grabbed him before he could land and Annie was holding him, his head in her lap. He said, "I love you" and drifted away into shadows...

They took Gray to the Emergency Room as soon as they could load him in the back of the restaurant van. It was Hank and Lewis the bartender and Bobby, a waiter, who had plowed into Dewey and his huge friend. According to Annie, she came through the door to witness his beating and had screamed for help and they had charged down the steps and attacked Dewey and his companion. Their discovery alone was probably what made the two run away but Annie said Hank hit the big guy like a defensive tackle for the Dallas Cowboys and was pounding him in the face even as Dewey was calling their retreat. They ran to a nondescript black import and drove off with Hank chasing them down the street. He was trying to read the license number but it was indecipherable. There was no light and the numbers were hidden by mud.

The ER doctor said Gray didn't have a concussion or broken bones and gave him a script for super ibuprofen and a cream that he said would help with the bruises. Then he sent them on their way. Gray had more bandages than visible skin and both eyes were blackened.

They met Beth and Hank at Denny's where they all had breakfast. After a few minutes Gray looked up to see Wagner coming to the table, his usual smile locked in place.

"Now Gray, this just has to stop" he patted him on the shoulder and hugged Annie and sat down with them. "Man, you look like you were hit by a truck" the old man said.

"I think it was a freight train" the musician laughed. "If it wasn't for Hank here I'd probably be in the hospital right now... or dead."

Hank laughed. "Don't blame it on me. I had lots of help." He had a black eye and a big bruise on the left side of his face.

"Maybe," Beth said, "but you hit the big guy like a tackle dummy. I think you should try out with the Cowboys. You have absolutely no sense. None. He could have killed you."

Hank grunted in pain. "Well I don't think he did. I hurt too much to be dead. God, what a monster he was. Who is he? Does anyone know?"

"The cops said they 'might have an idea or two.' They 'would get back to us.' You know how they are. They don't tell you anything until it's all over." Beth had done most of the talking with the police while everyone else had been busy getting first aid or going to the hospital with Gray. She had followed the guys out when Annie yelled and had watched the rescue from the steps.

Gray mostly listened as stories were told about the attack. He had limited experience available besides receiving heavy blows. But listening was an experience in itself. He had the strange feeling he had sat in this circle before listening to these stories told excitably or other stories like these, especially when listening to Hank. Maybe it was after an intramural boxing match. He couldn't quite remember. When Hank started yelling, he felt like he was in a bar after a brawl talking over a Saturday night victory. The feeling grew whenever Wagner asked questions, smiling like he'd never had more fun. He got chills down his back at one point and it waxed into the strongest déjà vu that he'd ever experienced. It was almost as if, for a split second, he was somewhere else in another group. Then he felt himself growing dizzy and things began to slip out of focus. He put his head in his hands and rested his elbows on the table. He noticed they were getting wet from something he had spilled.

"Hey" Annie said "are you OK darlin'? You're pale as a ghost."

"Sure, I'm fine" he said "I just feel tired."

"I think we need to get you home. The doctor said you should rest and take it easy."

"I think maybe you two should stay at our house until this is over." It was Beth as mother hen.

"Don't be silly." Annie said. "It's awfully nice of you to offer but you guys don't have room for us. You'd be ready to kill us or yourselves in a week."

"Well I have room for you two." Wagner interrupted. "Matter of fact, I have a whole house that you can have, with a view besides. It's the original settler's cabin that my great grandfather built in the 1850's, recently renovated with all the conveniences. You'll love it. You can go out right now if you want. I'll bring you your things later."

Beth said quickly "I'll do it. I want to help. You two go on."

Annie looked worried. "I don't think you should go by yourself. It seems that idiot really is dangerous. He could be watching my place."

"He has nothing against me. "Beth answered. "He doesn't know me from Queen Elizabeth. It will only take me five minutes; and I can see Wagner's wonderful ranch. All I need is a list of what to get."

"My guitar" Gray muttered.

"Yes, and your clothes etc." Annie was laughing. "Here honey, I'll write it all down."

26

## DÉJÀ VU

**G**ray and Annie followed Wagner through the wide open country of rolling limestone hills out to his ranch. They stopped at an impressive security gate while he entered the combination. Two rock columns of fieldstone were crowned by a black wrought iron arch bearing the name: The Linden Tree Ranch. Over the name an elaborate tree rose impressively in the same black wrought iron. The gate rose up from a six foot rock wall that stretched thirty feet on either side. The wall ended in a new four strand barbwire fence with metal fence posts that curved away out of sight in either direction. A well-maintained caliche drive stretched up the hillside ahead of them.

Annie grabbed Gray's forearm excitedly. "Wow! This place is magic."

The drive rolled through wide Hill Country pastures separated by cedar breaks and groves of live oaks. Everything looked as if it had been manicured that morning. Trees were trimmed and golden grasses waved in the chill north wind that rolled up the hills from the river. Herds of white tail deer and a few longhorns roamed the open fields and lent everything a sense of timelessness. After two left turns off the main drive they emerged onto a ridge with a wide view of the whole valley. The road passed below, largely hidden by the trees. The river stretched off to the southeast and disappeared into the folding green hills. A circling hawk defined the high curve of the pale winter sky. And at the crest of the ridge, shaded by great live oaks, there stood a house. It looked nearly organic, as if it had grown there forever. It was obviously old, like a large version of a pioneer cabin, but it looked well cared for and there was a tile roof instead of cedar shingles. Smoke trailed away from a limestone chimney, twisted into a long braid by the wind. Wagner pulled up into a circular drive and stopped beside a hedge of holly and got out of his truck. Gray and Annie parked behind him.

"Well kids, this is it, your home away from home. You have all the modern etc. except for TV, which you don't watch anyway. There is a good stereo and an extensive record collection, mostly classical. There's a wine rack with some nice labels and beer in the fridge. Help yourself to anything you..." Wagner was watching Gray as he spoke. Annie followed his eyes.

Gray was looking very unsteady, staring vacantly ahead and swaying on his feet. Annie quickly moved alongside of him and he sagged as she grabbed him. Wagner moved to his other side.

"Whoa, my friend let's get you inside where you can rest. You're not looking so well. I'm an old idiot. You need to get off your feet and I keep you here blabbing away. The master bedroom is upstairs and when you feel stronger you might move up there. It's a great room. But for now I've had Angel fix up the downstairs' bedroom. Your phones will work fine so you can check on things or call me. I've had the fridge and pantry stocked for you. Tomorrow, if you're feeling better, I hope you'll join me for dinner. Now I'll leave you to start healing. If you need anything call me." Annie got Gray comfortable and asked him if he needed anything.

"I need to get my head straight. I've never felt this weird in my life. It must be the pounding or the drugs or something but I keep expecting other people to come around the corner, people who aren't here. It's like déjà vu gone crazy. I start to answer questions that nobody asked. It's so strange" he muttered. A minute later he was sound asleep.

Annie looked out the window at the golden winter grass rippling across an open pasture in the wind. There was a peace here that seemed limitless. Nothing in the view indicated that Man had ever come here. There were no buildings, no cattle. A few deer grazed on the bright hillside. It all seemed to her like some perfect, miniature world encapsulated under a crystal dome. She felt that she could pick it up, and shake it and watch the snowflakes settle. That image was so strong that she had to shake her head to clear it and get her true perspective back.

# 27

# BETH

**B**eth stood in Annie's apartment wondering what else they might need. She'd gotten everything on the list, but the list was made in a rush. She got their tooth brushes and bathroom things but added Annie's shampoo and conditioner. She got her pajamas and then with a smile added a pretty negligee. She got Gray's guitar and added Annie's flute. The harp was just too big. She got two changes of clothes. She thought about calling and asking her if she wanted anything else but reminded herself that it wasn't for long and they weren't going to Alaska. Besides, from what she'd heard about Wagner's ranch, she and Hank might want to take a ride out so that he could see it too. She thought about how well she and Annie got along. She hadn't had many good friends. She never wanted to be "one of the girls". But Annie was so different from most women. She knew who she was without some guy around to define her. She worked part time even though she didn't have to. Annie's father would pay for everything but she wouldn't take an allowance. She was strong and independent like Beth herself. It seemed to her that most women, starting with her mother and her sister, weren't anyone unless their husbands were there to tell them who that was. Maybe that was a bit overstated but since her father had died her mother had seemed to melt away to grandmother and not much else. If it hadn't been for her sister and her kids she'd have nothing to do. And her big sister was following the same pattern. Oh, she and Hank wanted to have a child when the time was right, but for now they were busy building a business... and a life. And they wanted to spend time together, just the two of them. They wanted to get to know each other, without children around to interrupt the process. And Hank never tried to control her. As a matter of fact, he ran his kitchen and she ran everything else. And that was perfect. Of course, she hadn't known any of that when she first met him. She just knew that for some reason he was the one she wanted. He was big and good looking and very strong, but it was much more than that. It felt like he'd been away for a long time and she'd been really missing him. She would have married him if he hadn't had a cent, but as luck would have it, his parents were wealthy

She quit her gathering and took a load out to the car and put it in the back seat. Then she went back inside for the rest. She realized that she hadn't closed the drapes. It had been so dark she could hardly see anything in the living room. She understood why they closed it all up. Crazy people will make you nervous. But she couldn't have stood it. It made her claustrophobic. She looked around the apartment once more and didn't find anything else that it seemed they might need. She thought about how beautiful Annie's place was, how everything fit and how different it was from most student apartments. Then she left and locked the door behind her, both locks, and went out to her car. She'd parked out back because Annie told her to. There was an old blue van parked between her and her car. She thought a workman might be doing repairs. She noticed that the side door of the van was open but there was nobody around. She put the load in the back seat and closed the door and as she turned to the driver's door she heard a noise behind her in the van. She was turning to see what it was and something hit her in the back of her head and everything faded to black.

# 28

## THE SEARCH

It was nearly dark out and Annie was worried. Beth had never come with their things. She had called her cell phone but she didn't answer. She started to call Hank to check on the problem but she didn't have his number. She was about to call the restaurant when he called her.

"So Annie, is Beth still there? I've been trying to call her for an hour but her phone must not work out there."

Her heart sank and a shock of dread went down her spine. "No Hank. I've been trying to call her too. It goes right to voicemail. I expected her hours ago."

"Oh damn it! Annie you go drive the roads and see if she got lost or ran out of gas or something. I'll go to your place and see if I can pick up her trail. Stay in touch."

Annie called Wagner and told him what was going on. She asked him if he could come keep an eye on Gray because he was still passed out. The old rancher said he'd send Angel to watch over the patient but that he was going with Annie. He said it looked more and more like they were under attack and he wasn't letting her go alone. Minutes later he drove up in his truck. Angel got out and shook her hand and told her that she would "take good care of your boy". Then Annie got in with Wagner and he drove off in a hurry. They decided they would go to the main crossroads and turn away from the ranch to see if she had turned the wrong direction or had car trouble on the way. The road was deserted all the way to the junction. They were about to turn when Hank called.

"Annie, I'm at your place and her car is still here with all your stuff in it. I talked to your neighbors and they said the car was here when they got here but they saw no sign of Beth. I called the cops and they are on the way; so meet me here. OK?"

Annie said she was coming and told him where her extra key was hidden. Wagner called his ranch foreman and told him to put two men with rifles on the gate. He told him to tell the gate guards to park back from the road and out of sight; and he sent one to stay with Angel and Gray. He said, "I wouldn't worry too much about Beth, honey. I think she can handle anything that comes her way. Just a feeling I have from talking to her."

Annie put her hand on Wagner's arm. "I think you are right about Beth, Hans, but she got drawn into this because of me. I guess I misjudged Dewey badly. I really didn't think that he was dangerous and so I've put everyone in danger, Gray, Beth and Hank, even you and the people on your ranch."

The old man took her hand. "Don't you worry about me, love. I learned a long time ago that you are perfectly safe anywhere because there is destiny at work in every life. When your moment comes there's nothing that you can do to avoid it, but until then you can live totally unafraid. I've been in a thousand tight spots and I'm still here. I was at Anzio in WWII and fought in one campaign or another until VE Day. I was in Nigeria at a drilling site during a civil war once... oh never mind. I don't need to be telling war stories. The point is that if you don't waste your life on worry, if you live it instead, you don't need to dread its end. You will always be ready."

"You are a wise old man." Annie squeezed his hand. "Or else you're totally crazy. Do you know what bothers me most about all this? I feel so helpless. I'm not used to being helpless. Usually when I want something done it's done. I feel like I should be able to just make Dewey go away and leave us all alone. This time I tried but it didn't work."

Wagner nodded. "The thing is, none of us understand how much power we have. We are pure spirits who play a game of wearing bodies. We have limitations in this physical world because we choose to have them. If we knew who we really are... well, we could do anything. I think somehow that you were born knowing you were unlimited. Or, maybe we all are, but because you have a powerful and indulgent father, and through him a lot more power and freedom than most folks, you are just learning your self-imposed human limitations. That can be frightening. You aren't used to not getting your way."

"OK, now I know. You are totally crazy. No, I guess you're right. It doesn't make me sound very good though; does it? Just another spoiled little rich girl."

"No, that's not true. You're no spoiled brat. But I think that you chose this life because you would have power. Probably you were powerful before and you did well with it. You learned and were kind and helpful and generous. I know it doesn't sound like a rational, pragmatic, 20[th]century approach, but I believe it to be true all the same."

At Annie's there were police cars everywhere. Hank said that, normally, missing persons required twenty four hours before the police would act, but, due to the special circumstances with Dewey, they'd started right away. They had put out a report describing Beth, and both Dewey and the big guy that had jumped Gray. His name they found out, was John Slovensky, and he had a record of suspected but unproven crimes. His current address was directly across the street. It gave Annie chills. She looked up at the attic windows and wondered why she'd never felt anything. The police questioned her about Dewey and everything just like they had before and finally told her that she should go get some rest. They asked where she was staying and she said with a friend out of town and they suggested that she be very careful and watchful. And then they left, all of them. The neighbors all came over to talk and Annie had to explain the whole story again. Hank went back to the restaurant to see if there were any calls and wait by the phone. Annie asked him to come stay out with her and Gray but he said he wanted to stay close to home. Then she and Wagner went back to the ranch, riding all the way in silence.

# 29

## LIZARD

**H**er hands were tied to the saddle horn. The horse she rode was near the end of its strength and wheezed its unsteady way along the trail. The saddle was too big for her and chafed the inside of her thighs.

"My friends are going to like you a lot."

She was naked to the waist, her brother's shirt tied loosely about her belt. The Texas sun was burning the white skin that had seldom known its touch before. Soon it would blister. She was tethered to the scum who rode man-like on Charlemagne before her. Occasionally he would yank her rope and cause her to move up alongside him and he would make some loathsome jest and squeeze her breast or pinch her nipple. Her breasts were very tender from the pregnancy. Every time he touched them they hurt badly, but she showed him no sign. She was certain that if he knew it hurt her he would do it more often. They had ridden all morning towards Mason, on their way to meet his friends at some prearranged time and place. She had spat at him and cursed him the first few times he groped her and she had a bruised face and a split lip to show for it. Now she silently planned his death instead.

She still could not believe that she had been so careless. She had been riding for so long and she was so weary, weary beyond any imagining. Darkness had caught her out in open and she had fallen asleep and slipped to the ground and lay there. She knew she should rise and find some safe place to hide but she fell into unconsciousness instead. In the daylight she awoke to a kick in the ribs and opened her eyes to blinding morning sunlight silhouetting the outline of a man.

"So friend," he said, "what's a boy like you doin' way out here alone in the wilderness?"

There was something in his voice that was absolutely chilling. It was high and thin and wheedling. She started to jump and run but he kicked her hip and rolled her over and shoved a cocked forty-four in her face, her forty-four.

"Now that ain't a mannerly answer to a perfectly civil question, is it?"

He was very tall, over six feet, and rail thin, with several days growth of beard that was black with streaks of gray and some white. His neck was even skinnier than the rest of him and unnaturally long, and when he talked his Adam's apple bobbed up and down like some strange machine. She was terrified, but she forced her will to take control and she shook her head obligingly.

"Well, that's better little brother. Now stand up real slow and take off your boots and hand them to me."

Sara did as she was told, wondering why he wanted her to take her boots off.

One of his front teeth was broken and one was missing. His nose was long and thin and crooked, angling first right and then to the left. He looked like he hadn't changed his clothes since he bought them, if he bought them. And his smell was horrible, almost overpowering, like a dog smells when it rolls in something dead. She had never seen an uglier human.

He looked into each boot in turn. "Nope, no knives here, but they won't fit me either. My God you have little feet. How old are you, fourteen... no thirteen, am I right?"

Sara put on her best thirteen year old boy's voice. "Yes sir. I just turned thirteen last month."

"I knew it. Thirteen, how about that? And a German too, ain't ya?"

"Yes sir." The chill was growing stronger.

"Say something in German for me, would ya?"

Sara cursed his mother for giving him birth.

"That sounds real pretty. What did you say?"

"I wished you a good morning." Sara lied smiling.

"Well, good mornin' to you. So now, tell me, what's your name and what are you doing all alone out here?"

Sara thought quickly, trying to come up with a story that might help her. "My name is Jon. My Pa left for Mason two days ago. He's supposed to be back in a week but my mother is having a baby and it's coming early. She sent me to find Pa but I was really tired and I fell asleep. Please mister, let me go. My Ma needs me."

"Well, sure son. I'm gonna let you go. I just need your horse. I'm sorry, but mine broke his foreleg back a ways. I borrowed the one I got from some old white-headed Indian but it's almost as dead as him. Funny thing, though, he didn't want to give him up. I should've rode the Indian and killed the horse." He cackled at his joke.

"Well, look at me, getting careless again" he said in his lizard voice. "I need to make sure you aren't carrying any other weapons. I just want to be certain. You understand. Take off your clothes, all of them. Now. And throw them over here."

He moved back two paces and watched her, smiling his lizard smile.

Sara turned around, acting like she was unbuttoning her shirt and then she just started running. She didn't know what to do but run, though she knew there was no place for her to go.

"Now don't do like that. Come back here. We're gonna have a good time." Lizard man mounted up on Charlemagne and raced up alongside her as she ran. He was laughing and whooping. "Come on now son, I've taught lots of boys how the cow ate the cabbage. Some of them even liked it." Then he turned the big horse into her path and she fell and rolled. He dismounted and straddled her, grabbing her wrists and pinning her to the ground. The grass was high and yellow and it irritated her face and neck. She fought for her freedom but he was very strong. There was no way. Eventually she quieted.

"There you are. Smart boy. Sometimes, however you feel about things, you just got to go along. Now…"
he said, moving back and drawing his gun, "Get those clothes off."

She took off her trousers and started to unbutton the shirt. "Drawers too boy." He said with a look halfway between a grimace and a leer. She started to turn around but he said "None of that."

Then, trembling, slowly, she pulled down her underwear.

'Well would you look at that, he ain't no boy after all. Hmm, hmm, well I was willing to make do, but see how my luck has changed. Now then ma'am," he said, exaggerating the word, "why don't you take off the rest."

Suddenly the sky wheeled over her head, and Sara passed out of consciousness and floated down into a dark, deep hole. When she came back to herself he was lifting her up into the saddle of his dying horse and cursing. Her pants were back on but not her shirt or her carefully arranged binding that kept her breasts concealed. It lay on the ground nearby along with her brother's drawers. She hurt everywhere, but she remembered nothing of what had happened after she fainted. She thanked her fate for that pardon and began the long, hot ride to the lizard's rendezvous, considering her rapist's death with every step that the shambling wreck of a horse took. All her energy, all her being, was focused on a single intent. He had to die. She would not be afraid and she would not die and she would not stop until he was dead. He had to die.

# 30

## PRISONER

All day as they rode through the hills, her mind raced furiously from one plan to the next. What could she do? What? But her furious questioning and planning remained fruitless and her despair, always at the edge of her consciousness, threatened to swallow her. Then she would call back her anger, fierce and horrible and dark. She didn't yet know what to do, but she did know that she would die before she let him use her again.

He was humming some tuneless song as he rode. He constantly reigned in Charlemagne because her old Indian pony was moving slower with every mile. She'd expected the horse to collapse at any time, but he surprised her, stubbornly following Charlemagne's lead across the hills, wheezing and lurching as he went. The lizard had tired of his groping jests and had switched to vivid descriptions of the "great time" she would have when they met up with his friends.

The sun was setting in a pool of blood when the lizard called their camp site. They had followed the line of the trail as they rode, but shadowing it half a mile to the north. The place he chose was screened from the trail by a juniper grove. Though he said nothing, his fear of meeting other travelers was apparent. His eyes searched the road constantly, ahead and behind. She wondered if it was because of her or because others were trailing him. Either way his caution lessened any chance of rescue.

Then, as she rode into the clearing, she saw her chance, small and dangerous, but a chance. There in the dust below her was a rock. It was slightly larger than her hand. To most eyes it was pretty unimpressive, but she recognized it from her childhood days when she and her little brother had combed their father's paddocks searching for arrowheads. It was an Indian scraper carved from chert, a kind of stone related to flint but not as brittle or shiny. It was a tool used to scrape animal hides. It had a very sharp edge and was shaped to fit the hand. They came in many sizes, depending on the stone and the job they were needed for. This was a large one. How her eyes managed to lock their gaze on the shaped stone she could not explain. There it was just the same, the only thing in her field of vision.

As soon as the lizard untied her from her saddle he grabbed her wrist. But she slipped from her horse on the opposite side, kicking him as she went. At the same time she kicked the pony in the ribs. He lurched forward a few steps but remained between her and the outlaw. Using her weight and gravity to break his bruising grip, she slipped to the ground. She stumbled purposefully and palmed the scraper as invisibly as she could, slipping it into her trouser pocket. Then she began to run for the cedar thicket. Before she got ten feet he caught her from behind, knocking her to the ground and reaching for her wrists. She rolled over and drove her knee into his groin and when he hesitated and grunted in pain she grabbed the scraper from her pocket and drove it into his forehead as brutally as she could. She hoped to knock him out or stun him. Instead, she opened up a bloody groove from his left eye socket through the bridge of his nose and into his right eyebrow. Then she sprinted for the dense cedar growth across the clearing and plunged in. He was behind her in an instant, mopping at the blood flow with a filthy handkerchief and screaming at her in his high, strange voice.

"You blinded me you whore! You'll pay for it too. God damn you bitch, you get your ass back here now!"

She kept pressing further into the cedar, her legs and body shaking uncontrollably. She could barely make her muscles obey her will.

"I'm telling you, you'll be sorry. I'll hurt you so bad you'll beg to die." He had come to the edge of the bramble and was peering in at her past his ragged bandage. "I can see you, you stupid slut. In ten seconds I'm going to start shooting. Get back here now!"

She squirmed always deeper into the almost impenetrable brush, raking her bare body as she went. She knew she was about to die but it seemed almost a blessing to her now... except for the life she carried in her womb. Bleeding and terrified, she prayed to a god she had always said did not exist. "If you are there Great One, if you do care for us as we struggle and die, help me and my child now. She longs to live. I feel it. And I long to hold her in my arms. Please..."

Suddenly, as she pushed into the gathering shadows she heard a loud voice speaking, booming, deep and resonant. "Don't be afraid ma'am. It's over. You can come out now. Your deliverance has come. The Lord be praised."

"Who is it?" she answered, her voice breaking and trembling, "Who are you?" She trusted no one, nothing, at this point, deliverer or not.

"Ma'am, I am grateful to be Brother Mordecai Yell, the humble servant of the Lord God. I'm the Methodist circuit rider for this territory, on my way west to Menard before I head back home. I have been trailing the Weasel for three days. He killed a friend of mine and stole his horse and I followed him to send him to the fiery gates of Hell where he belongs."

"Weasel?" she asked, "Who is he?"

"He is the loathsome, foul-smelling villain who pursued you. Who, I'm sure you will be relieved to know, is now unconscious in a pile at my feet with my shotgun at his neck. It is, therefore, safe for you to come out now."

And she began to weep and shiver. The sense of relief was too powerful for her to endure. Her mind began to circle over her head like a bird, above the treetops. She could see herself weeping and weeping and shrinking into a small bundle of exhaustion in the cedar break and a large man crashing through the brush to reach her. He was saying in a warm, kind voice Ma'am, Ma'am? It's all right Ma'am. It's all right. It's all right, reaching her and picking her up in strong arms and carrying her through the branches to the clearing where he covered her with his coat and pillowed her head with a bedroll while her mind left its circling and flew away to a great height and brightening clouds, wonderful clouds...

# 31

## MORDECAI YELL

**W**hen she awoke it was midmorning. A campfire was burning and lending the bright smell of cedar wood to the smell of coffee waiting. Then it came back to her like a slap, everything that had happened over the last two days. She sat up startled and looked around her. There, across the clearing and out in the open beyond the cedar break cover, in plain view of the road, stood the lizard. His hands were tied behind his back and he was tethered to an oak tree. Before him stood a very large man in a black frock coat and trousers, wearing a black, flat-brimmed hat with a low crown. He wore a black vest and a string tie and a white shirt. In his hands he held a book and he was talking to the lizard. The lizard saw her movement and turned to look at her with a foul smirk on his bloody ruin of a face. The big man followed his gaze and began walking toward her smiling a warm, kind smile. He was huge, over six and a half feet tall, with arms and legs like tree trunks. He came to the fire and bent over and poured out a cup of coffee which he handed to her.

"Good morning. I'm afraid the coffee's not very good but at least it's a lot better than my cooking. Welcome back to the world. I tried to tend to your hurts as well as I could with the salve my wife puts on everything. I don't know how much you remember from yesterday, but my name is Mordecai Yell. I'm a Methodist traveling preacher, a circuit rider they call us, working the West Texas Conference. Well, actually, I'm not circuit riding anymore. Now I'm the Presiding Elder. The frontier has been "tamed", the Conference decided, and it's time to assign regular pastors. Now I conduct quarterly conferences with different congregations. It feels the same to me. I'm going all the way to the Menard fellowship before I head home to my family near Austin. Yell Settlement they call it, to my embarrassment, but I couldn't persuade my neighbors otherwise."

"What will you do with him?" she asked, nodding at the lizard. "You won't let him go..."

"The Weasel? Oh no, I won't let him go. Before you and I leave this clearing we are going to hang him from the tree he's standing under. Soon he will go before the Lord, who will judge him fairly, even with tender mercy, and still he will be attended by the Devil tonight. He is a very evil man. I think you know."

"His name is Weasel? I always thought of him as the lizard."

"I fear we do both species a grave injustice. But Weasel is how he's known across East Texas and the Hill Country as long as I've known of him. Where he comes from or what he was christened, I doubt if even he remembers. He has destroyed lives and broken hearts and murdered the defenseless and raped and tortured and committed such cruelty that no one but the Comanche can be called his equal, and perhaps not even they."

"You said you were a preacher," she said. "Are you a lawman too?"

"No ma'am. I represent no law but the law of God. But this foul carrion killed a friend of mine two days ago to get that old Indian pony over there. In a few hours we were to meet and when he didn't come on time I rode out to find him." Yell's mouth set in a grim line and anger flashed in his eyes.

"He said he killed an old white-haired Indian to get it." She said, confused. "He said the Indian didn't want to give it up."

"Yes, that's right. My friend was Ado Tainte, White Tree, a Kiowa medicine chief. The horse was his medicine horse. It's very old. White Tree and I wanted to talk about the Kiowa giving up the war trail. Most had already done it but there were still hotheads riding with the Comanche, small groups. They're still causing a lot of grief to my members from time to time. We were friends for twenty years, he and I, ever since I saved him from a bunch of miners who had him by his old hair and were about to scalp him. They were mostly heathens but one of their leaders was my Methodist. White Tree was old even then. Later he talked a Comanche raiding party out of scalping me. He told them that I was a medicine man and I would curse anyone who caused my death. They let me go unmolested. I worked these circuits for so many miles, so many years... It was good to have friends. The Lord God rules."

"Did you always know that God would take care of you? Don't you get scared?"

Mordecai grinned. "Sure I do. That's what these Colts are for." He patted the handles of two pistols, one holstered on either side of his body…" "and my shotgun." Then he excused himself and walked over to the lizard. He talked to him again and read from the bible, the book that he was carrying.

Suddenly the lizard laughed, a horrible, high-pitched wheezing that sounded like Death laughing. Then the preacher brought the old pony over to the oak tree where a lariat was strung across a heavy bough. Sara drew close. He set the noose around the outlaw's neck and picked up the lizard and set him in the saddle, though he was a large man, though he kicked and fought and cursed and screamed. Mordecai Yell picked him up over his head and set him in the saddle. She was amazed. And the pony stood unmoving as granite, though the screams were nearly enough to make Sara bolt.

Yell removed his hat, letting it hang down his back by its cord. His steel-gray hair hung to his shoulders. He pulled the rope tight and tied it off. Then he turned to the cedar a few feet away and broke off a branch and stripped it of needles and handed it to Sara. "Your quirt ma'am."

Sara hesitated, and stood looking at the switch in his hand, but he made no move until she took it from him. Then he turned back to the Weasel on his horse and spoke in a deep, sonorous voice. "Weasel, you who are known as the Weasel, whatever your Christian name, you now ride to your death, confronted by your accuser, the witness to your crimes, your victim, and finally your executioner. You have been judged by me and found guilty before the Lord and the Lord now awaits you for judgment. Yet even now, at this late hour, you might be saved from eternal damnation by the Lord God's merciful forgiveness. Will you repent?"

The lizard's Adam's apple moved rapidly up and down and he cleared his throat. Then his lip twisted in a sneer and he spat at the judge below him.

The preacher stood unmoving, stern and unassailable beside the horse.

"Then, villain, have you any last words?"

Weasel turned his head to look into Sara's eyes. She saw the smirk play across his face again and then he said, "Hit her hard bitch. I'm ready to get out of this hell hole."

Mordecai said, in an almost jovial tone, "It may be that you will change your mind when you face the real thing."

"And it may be I'll spit in the Devil's eye, preacher man. And God damn you all, you wretched hypocrites. God damn you all!" His voice rang out clearly in the glade.

Sara brought the branch down on the horse's buttocks and the pony shot forward as if it were a two year old colt and left its rider kicking at the air. She continued to watch until all movement ended. Then she walked back to the fire and stood shuddering as if from cold. Yell followed her and, standing behind her, placed his great hands on her shoulders. She turned to face him and, leaning against his broad chest, she began to weep.

# 32

# THE ROOM

**W**hen Beth woke up she tried to understand why she was bound. Then she saw a faint light and realized that she was blindfolded as well. She was lying on a bed. It was an old bed. It smelled very musty and the springs squeaked when she moved. Her hands were bound behind her and her feet were taped at the ankles. There was a strip of tape across her mouth. She could hear a man talking. It was muffled and she couldn't tell what he was saying but she could tell that it was an argument over the phone. The place smelled of mold and mildew. The sound of rushing water was very loud. She had no idea where she was but it seemed obvious that whoever held her had something to do with Dewey, Annie's curse. She had a really bad headache. She thought, "Damn it, Annie told me not to go alone. Why didn't I listen to her? Why did Hank let me go?" She knew, though, that everyone was caught up in Gray's beating and the fight and the emergency room. No one was paying close attention, including her. She had only herself to blame. Then she started trying to think of the best thing she could do. Her first thought was to get herself free. She began to struggle against the bonds but soon decided that it was hopeless. It was some kind of tape, probably duct tape, but wrapped many times and impossible to break or even stretch. The voice stopped talking and she heard him curse. Then the light brightened a little. He must have opened a door wider because the sound of the water got louder as well. She heard him walking toward her, his steps loud on a concrete floor. He knelt down beside the bed, breathing heavily. Then he ran his hands over her, groping her, feeling the contours of her body. He unbuttoned the top three buttons on her blouse and slipped his hand inside her brassiere and cupped her breasts and played with her nipples. And she became steel. She wasn't afraid. She knew she would win. She knew it as if it were a movie she'd already seen and she was just watching it again.

"So he says don't even touch her until he gets here. Like he's so high and mighty. He says he's mad because I didn't wait for him to snatch you like I was supposed to. He doesn't care that I saw a perfect chance to pick you up. I did it all by myself. Why should I have to let him have you first? I caught you. You're mine to do with what I want."

But she could tell that he was losing his argument. He was backing down.

"I know he's not going to call the cops. He'd be in it too if he did; I don't care what he says. He just has to always run things. I'm sick of it. I should just kick his ass. That's what I should do. God damn it. That would be easy. He's a punk." Then he buttoned her blouse up and went out slamming the door and bringing total darkness. She heard him fastening a padlock and she listened to his footprints moving away. But it was only moments before the sound of his steps was drowned out by the rush of the water so she couldn't tell how far he had gone.

She began immediately to work on the blindfold. By moving her head back and forth against the mattress she managed to make it come loose and scraped it off onto the bed. Without the blindfold she noticed that there was a faint glow coming in from under the door. She felt better now that she could see a little, even though it was still dark, and she tried to study her surroundings in the dim light. She could tell that the room was small, that it had concrete walls, that it had a low ceiling. There was a large rectangular object against the corner beside the door... a desk? And in front of the desk and her bed was a chair. She had to get free before he came back. She couldn't think of a way to free her wrists but she knew how to get rid of the tape around her ankles. She went to yoga class once a week- every Thursday afternoon. She bent backwards in the bow pose and brought her ankles to her hands. Her fingers were numb from lack of circulation but they were free. She clenched and unclenched her hands to make them more functional. She searched for the edge of the tape by scraping it with her fingernail. She located it over her right ankle bone and scraped it until she could get the end between her fingers. By pulling it straight across she freed a strip about six inches long. It was a slow process but soon her legs were free.

She sat up and put her feet on the floor and breathed, deep and slow, for a minute. Then she stood up and moved to the desk. It was an old fashioned industrial metal desk. The surface was dust-covered and rusty. Then she heard footsteps coming. She threw herself back on the bed and hastily arranged the tape around her ankles so that in the dim light it might go unnoticed. She could hear him fumbling with the lock and then he came in.

The room flooded with daylight. She lay still, feigning sleep, but she watched him from under her nearly closed eyelids long enough to recognize him as the big man who had beaten Gray so badly. His face bore the bruises from her husband's blows. He grunted and picked up her blindfold from beside her head and put it back on her. She acted like she was waking up and moaned into her duct tape gag, as if she were trying to talk to him.

He said "It's not a good idea for you to take off your blindfold. It wouldn't be good for you to see us. I don't want anything bad to happen to you. I just want to mess around a little. Don't make it a big deal."

Then he started tugging at her blouse and began unbuttoning it. This time he unbuttoned it all the way down. She never moved. She told herself that she couldn't do anything, so she lay still and concentrated on not reacting. She didn't want him to know she had freed her ankles. When he opened her blouse he pulled her bra straps down on her shoulders, freeing her breasts. He fondled them with both hands. Then he ran his hand over her stomach and down into her pants and into her underwear. He slipped his fingers over her hair and rubbed it softly, moaning under his breath. She began to lose control. Her skin crawled. She had never understood that it was a real sensation. It had never happened to her before. Her muscles were shuddering on their own. She suddenly realized that if he was aroused enough, his fear of his accomplice would no longer protect her. Her body was threatening to throw up. She blocked that impulse with a powerful command of will. With her mouth taped shut she could choke to death. She wondered if she could get around him and run, but that was stupid. She was blindfolded and had her hands tied. Suddenly there was a huge gust of wind, out of nowhere. It blew the door all the way open and banged it back and forth against the inside wall, making an enormous clamor and startling her captor away from his intentions. Water blew into the room in a stinging spray and he stood up cursing and moved to secure the door. She heard him yelling. "What the fuck is going on?" and the door slammed closed and she heard the lock slip into place and she was alone in the dark again.

She waited a long time and he didn't come back. The wind quieted down again. For a while it had whistled and rattled the door but now it had stopped and there was only the muffled sound of the water rushing. She was wet now, and cold and she hoped she wouldn't get sick. But she rubbed off her blindfold once more and sat back up. After a minute just breathing through her nose to quiet her nerves, she got to her feet and went to the desk again. She opened the wide shallow drawer at the top as far as it would open. Then she systematically searched the drawer with her fingers, turning backwards and leaning against the desk. She nearly fell over a few times but she figured out how to balance herself leaning over backwards. She found nothing except the rusted remains of a few paperclips. She managed to open the top drawer on the side and did the same thing. Nothing. The bottom drawer was the most difficult but using the chair and the desk she managed to search it too. And she found something. She wasn't sure what it was at first but after much study decided it was the remains of an old metal file or rasp. It had a thin pointed end and then a long flat section. The rough part was lost to rust but it had a couple sharp spots caused by the rust crumbling away. She held it in place by sitting on it on top of the desk and extending it over the side. Then she used it to saw through the tape at her wrists. It took a while but finally her hands were free and she stripped off the tape that gagged her. She wanted to scream in exaltation but just babbled and prayed and whistled with joy for a moment in celebration and breathed through her mouth. It was wonderful. Then she straightened her bra and buttoned her shirt again and turned her attention to studying the door. She found the doorknob and turned it but there was no mechanism to work. She opened it until the lock stopped it. There was a padlock in a hasp that rattled when she tried it. But it was solid. There was no give at all, so she turned her attention to the room, looking for any tool that might help. She turned over the ruin of a mattress and examined the rusty springs. Nothing. She wondered where she was, what this place was.

Suddenly she heard footsteps outside again. She grabbed the file off the desk and stepped behind the door. It was the big man again. He said "What the hell" and then he swung the door open and saw her behind it. His left hand was still on the doorknob. His right hand was at his side. She didn't stop to think. She drove the rusty file into the soft flesh beneath his sternum. She held it in both hands and she shoved it up into his heart. The look on his face was pure surprise, which slid into disappointment and sadness and then he collapsed and died. Blood pooled out onto the floor. He lay on his back. His eyes were open and the look of sadness was frozen on his face.

Beth began to shake and sob. She sank down and leaned against the wall crying, her eyes closed against the World. And then a voice said, "Well, that is a shame. The dumb son of a bitch got the wrong woman." She opened her eyes to see Dewey standing there surveying the scene. She'd never seen Dewey clearly but she knew it was him. He was dark and really good looking. He looked arrogant and cold and absolutely insane. In his hand he held a pistol and it was aimed at her head.

# 33

## SISTERDALE

It was a bright morning and the sky climbed higher than she had seen it in weeks. It was the brightest blue she'd seen since she last saw Bethie's eyes. Mordecai rode ahead of her and as usual he was singing.

They were somewhere south of Luckenbach. They had stayed two nights with a Methodist German family named Decker in Sisterdale. They were old friends and parishioners of Brother Yell. The husband, whose name was Gustav, but who called himself Gus, was a big blonde, serious man, a deacon in Mordecai's congregation. The woman, whose name was Gertrude but who introduced herself as Gertie, was a strong, happy woman in her late thirties or early forties. She immediately took Sara into her heart and gave her a hot bath and a new set of clothes and a great, hot dinner. The house was well kept and very civilized, with hardwood floors and four bedrooms, two upstairs, and pictures on the wall. Four pretty children, two boys and two girls, all younger than eight years old, ran around noisily, excited at having company. Gus called a halt for dinner and they became perfect citizens for the rest of the evening.

Dinner was delicious. Gertie served jagerschnitzel, veal cutlets with mushroom gravy, one of Sara's favorites. There were fat dumplings, two kinds of potatoes and sausages and stewed apples for desert. There was strong coffee with sugar and thick cream. After starving on the trail all those days it was like having dinner in heaven for Sara.

There was a piano in the sitting room. After dinner, Gertie played music and they all sang, even the children. She played an old song that Sara hadn't heard since she was a child. It was called "the Linden Tree." She loved it and would make her mother sing it as a lullaby when she sang her to sleep. It made her terribly homesick for her mother and her own girls. She wanted so badly to go home that tears ran down her face from the corners of her eyes. Mordecai rose from his chair and sat beside her on the settee, putting his great hand on her back and patting her. He sang in a marvelous full baritone, and surprisingly, knew all of the German lyrics. He sang so gently and patted her so reassuringly, that she leaned against his shoulder and fell asleep. She came half-awake when he laid her in a huge, soft bed where Gertie fussed over her and helped her into a white flannel nightgown.

It was afternoon before she woke. Gertie was bringing breakfast on a tray, eggs and sausages, potato pancakes and a mug of fresh, steaming coffee laced with cream and chocolate.

"We need to get back your strength. Preacher told us you've had a very hard time. I'll let you eat. Just call if you need anything."

Sara quickly objected. "No, please don't go. Sit and talk a little."

Gertie pulled a chair up close to the bed and smiled. "Mordecai says you are going home to Mason?"

"Not really. Well, I am going to Mason, and it is my home, but I'm going back to find my... My children are in New Braunfels with my parents..." She stumbled, trying to find a way to say it and then, gave up and began to cry. Gertie moved to her side and tried to comfort her, but the tears wouldn't stop.

Gertie shushed her and patted her, and hugged her until she finished. "Just tell me sweetie. I promise that I won't be shocked. I have seen and done many things I wish I hadn't had to do. We all do, don't we?"

And Sara just started talking, stumbling over words and crying but eventually telling the whole story from Henry to Hans, to the mistake and the pregnancy and the letter and her desperate journey. She went on and on saying, all the things she didn't want to think about, much less speak about, until she got to the Lizard and her rescue by Mordecai Yell.

Her hostess hugged her. "You've been very brave and you've done amazing things for a young woman. And you have no reason to be ashamed. Life sneaks up on us sometimes, threatening all the things we once believed important and we do what we have to do to survive, and sometimes we conquer. But always luck has as much to do with it as anything else.

"When I was a young girl of fifteen, my father and mother brought my brothers and sister and me to Texas as part of the Adelsverein, the first German immigration. We landed at Indianola, on the coast in the fall. There were a lot of people. Wagons were supposed to bring us to the Hill Country. But they had started the Mexican War and the soldiers needed all the wagons. We were caught on the coast, just standing on the beach. Winter came and people started running out of money. My father did too. Everything was so expensive. We had no place to live. My father bought a tent early but many people were digging holes in the sand to live in- just to get out of the wind. It was very cold, even in our tent it was very cold. There was no wood for fires sometimes. There were no big trees, just bushes really. It rained all the time so what wood there was stayed wet. Everyone collected driftwood to burn but there was never enough. People started dying of starvation and sickness... Then the cholera started. All my family died- first my mother, then my brothers and then my sister. My father and I buried them in the sand. Then one morning I woke up and I was alone. My father had left in the night. I thought he went looking for food but later some people told me that at first light he had started wading out into the ocean. When he was deep enough he started swimming straight out and the sea took him. And I was alone. I was fifteen. I walked up to the ships and I asked someone if they would take me back to Germany. I thought I could find my grandmother. The men laughed and said no, that I was being silly. Then this old man in a nice suit said he would pay for my passage to Galveston if I would stay in his cabin with him. I was starving and cold and alone, so I did. When we got to Galveston he took me to a place, a brothel, and I stayed there for almost two years. The woman who owned the place was kind and I ate well and that is where I met Gus. He kept coming to see me every Friday and one night he asked me to marry him. I told him I couldn't, that I wasn't a good woman. He told me I was a very good woman; I had just done bad things because I had no choice. And he told me that he loved me, that he didn't care what I'd done, and he's never stopped loving me since." She hugged Sara once more and smiled a huge warm smile. "You see, love, whatever bad happens, it just happens. You have to know that good things will happen too."

After hearing Gertie's story, Sara began to feel better. The food and the coffee revived her, and almost immediately she decided it was time to get back to her journey. She got up and got dressed and went looking for the preacher. She didn't find Mordecai but she found Gertie. Her new friend was comforting crying children and trying to peel potatoes at the same time. Sara took over the potatoes.

"You don't need to be doing this. You should be resting." Gertie protested.

"If I sleep anymore they'll think I'm dead and bury me" Sara said. "Besides, I need to get back on the road. I have to find Hans. Where is Reverend Yell?"

"He and Gus are off visiting with the congregation. They're going to have a service tonight. I think it will be his last one as pastor. They are supposed to send us a new preacher any day now, a permanent one. Mordecai is actually the Elder now. He's been promoted. Mordecai says that you should rest and then rest some more. He says you still have a long way to go. And he's right." Gertie knew that Sara meant to leave right away and she knew why. She tried to talk her out of it. "If you wait for him it might take extra time but you'll be much safer.

He's been riding this road for years. He was supposed to be replaced after two years but I think it's been nearly ten. He's both wise and strong, a very good man. Wait Sara. We only think we choose our journey. Sometimes all we can really decide is how we react to what happens."

The night was interesting. They were good people and Mordecai's sermon was like him- strong and kind. It was the first religious service she had ever attended and she felt like a spy. Good people or not, Mordecai or not, she was glad when it was over.

When she and the preacher left in the morning she felt relieved. The need to find Hans was building in her every day. She was terrified that something might happen to him and leave Clara without a name. And there was something else. Watching Gus and Gertie together, happy and loving, made her realize how much she missed that closeness. And when she thought of Hans she knew that she loved him. She had never thought about it until her mother pronounced the words so clearly on the porch in New Braunfels. "Oh darling, you're in love with him." She hadn't stopped thinking about it since. She knew it was true. It felt strange to think of him that way. They had been friends since she first met Henry at a barn dance. She had danced with them both but only Henry asked for another dance. Hans went outside and drank beer and smoked his pipe with the men. After that Henry called all the time. Her mother thought he was too old for her, but her father liked him and thought his solid character would make a good husband. It was all decided before Henry ever proposed. She was excited by the idea of making a home on the frontier and he was so strong and big and good looking. And he was kind, very kind- and quiet with her. They would talk far into the night their first few years, about everything, about how many children they would have. He wanted a big family, but he said, since she had to do all the work, she should decide. And about the trip they would take to Germany. And he was a freethinker too.

She shook her head vigorously. She couldn't think about Henry. It still hurt too much. But she wondered if, through all those years of loving him, if she hadn't been in love with Hans as well. There had never been one sign from him and she hoped not from her, but looking back, she could see that as close as he was to Henry, and always there and having meals together and going to the markets, and parties and…

Well, was he just a friend? Did she love him only as a friend? Now she wondered. But now it didn't matter. Henry was gone and she loved Hans and she could lose him too.

Mordecai said the ride to Luckenbach was straight and easy. It was only sixteen miles and with Mordecai riding beside her, she wouldn't even be nervous. They could go all the way to Fredericksburg. It was only ten miles farther, but that would make it a hard ride. Besides, the preacher had to meet with the Luckenbach minister in his new job as Presiding Elder. Unlike Sisterdale, Luckenbach had their permanent appointee already.

The rest and grain had done Charlemagne a lot of good. He was throwing his head and snorting and shuffling his legs and she could feel the energy rippling through his muscles from the moment she mounted. He wanted to get back to the trail as badly as she did. As soon as they were clear of town she let him have his head and gallop for half a mile. When the preacher caught up he was clearly impressed.

He said "As long as you're mounted I won't have to worry about you. Nobody could catch you."

She felt better than she had since she received the letter from Hans. She told herself that she was riding to meet Hans and Beth and Annie and she knew that it was true. The trail stretched away under blue Texas skies toward the ever-beckoning hills and she joined Mordecai in his song.

# 34

## WAGNER'S DREAM

Gray woke up groaning, his body in pain. He didn't remember much about what had happened but he didn't really need to. The memory of his beating was written on his ribs and stomach, his kidneys and face. He'd been in many fights in his life but was never hurt this badly before. Of course, he thought, this wasn't really a fight. It was just a beating.

Wagner sat across the room in a big chair by the door. He was nodding, with an open book in his lap, the ever-present smile lost in sleep. Just as Gray was about to slip back into pain-free unconsciousness, Wagner yelled incoherently and sat up, dropping the book he was holding onto the floor.

Wide awake again, Gray raised his head painfully and looked across at his friend. "Wagner, are you OK?"

The old man's clear blue eyes were open wide, and a startled look held the normally peaceful features. Visibly collecting himself, Wagner met Gray's look. "Just a dream, son, I was only dreaming." His Texas drawl sounded thicker and more pronounced than usual. "Sorry if I woke you. How do you feel?"

"I'm hurting like hell. I must need more of those magic pills. What time is it, anyway?"

Wagner was smiling again. "It's two in the afternoon. Well past time for you to take more magic. Annie went to help Hank at the restaurant. He's having a really tough time... as you might expect. There's been no word from the police about Beth. I said I'd stay with you and keep you company."

Gray pulled himself up into a sitting position. He was trying to get his pillows into place for a backrest, because the great old headboard was elaborately carved black walnut and beautiful, but it was miserably uncomfortable to lean on. Wagner came over to help him out. "My great-grandmother's first husband carved that in the 1850's. My mother said that he came from a family of famous wood carvers in Germany." The headboard depicted an eagle, open-winged against a backdrop of rolling Texas hills. A great buck stood guard over his doe and her fawn. A small herd of buffalo was grazing on a hillside. "It's pretty but it doesn't make a great backrest. That's the reason it's not upstairs in the master bedroom."

After his benefactor had given him his meds and brought him fresh water, he turned to leave. Gray called him back. "Tell me something, will you Wagner? If we all live again and again, and we keep multiplying the numbers of humans on earth, then where do all the extra people come from? It seems like there ought to be a set number of people that cycle through. Why is the population constantly expanding?"

"No my friend, you have the wrong idea. All of this is a play. You know- Shakespeare? The great Creation who produces all this, the playwright if you will, just keeps dividing into more fragments to fit the evolving story. We are all pieces of the same great unity and that unity is infinite." Wagner looked positively beatific with wisdom.

"Well OK then, Mr. Guru, why would we keep returning to the creation? He has, or It has, infinite choices to create an endless supply of new characters. Why repeat me or you or anybody?" Gray wanted to understand but it seemed an over-complicated answer to a simple question.

The old man chuckled. "Because you see, as a character in this play, you haven't resolved all your issues. Or we haven't resolved what is between us, or whatever. That's what my defini-tion of Karma is- the resolution of all the story lines, tying up all the loose ends. The Universe hates loose ends. When they play out, then we return to the One, the Light, Nirvana. Or use a musical analogy, since you're a musician: this is a great Symphony and we are themes that return again to the music, a repetitive phrase, and when our part is finished we return to the Silence, the Unity that the music spills out of. Or switch to physics for your handle. What existed before the ever-expand-ing Universe, the Big Bang? Nothing. The Great Unity. The Stillness. The Silence. Do you see?"

Gray was shaking his head. "I don't know. I mean I think that I understand what you're getting at but I'll need to give it some thought."

"Good idea son. Here, take this and read it some time." And he handed Gray the book he'd been reading. "Long ago a friend of mine, an Indian driller named Ram, gave me that book. It's the Bhagavad Gita, one of the great books of the Vedanta, the Hindu scriptures. He told me to "read it some-time". We were opening an oil field in Nigeria and things got rough. We wound up in the middle of a turf war between local power groups, and twice we were virtually under siege. I thought we were dead. We were playing poker to pass the time. My friend never broke a sweat. He just kept playing poker and laughing, and raising on lousy hands and yelling "Melacamo!" which, in one of the hundreds of Nigerian languages, means "life is sweet"! I don't even know how it's spelled. That's the way he wrote it in a letter years later- Melacamo! Anyway, after I decided that I didn't want to work oil fields anymore, I remem-bered that time with Ram and I got out the book and I read it. And that's how an unbelieving Methodist became a heretical Hindu thirty-five years ago. That's just my take on it, by the way. Don't hold Ram responsible."

Gray thanked him for the book and was about to settle into the pillows to read it when Wagner spoke again. The old man was sitting in the big chair again and he had his head laid back and his eyes closed.

"You know that dream I had? You were in it, and so was that time in Nigeria. I was down hiding behind the rim of a berm. It's like a deep ditch that circles a storage tank. Anyway, I was by myself and there were a bunch of crazy-mad locals going to kill me and I was shooting at them over the edge of the berm and I knew I was about to get killed and you came driving up in a jeep with some other guy I didn't know and the two of you were shooting and screaming and you ran the whole damned bunch of them off. I mean, I know that's crazy, but your friend kept hugging me and yelling Melacamo! And after I woke up I had the damnedest sensation of déjà vu. And then you started talking about reincarnation... oh, I don't know. All that came back to me. The memory of Nigeria and my dream, they both seemed real. They had equal weight. Do you see what I mean? They both seemed like a memory. It's just wonderfully strange. There was more to the dream but that's the part that you were in."

Gray cleared his throat. "Speaking of déjà vu, ever since we got here I've been going nuts. At first I thought it was from the beating or the drugs but it hasn't stopped. If anything, it's getting stronger.

I know everything about this place- how the walls were built, hell, how the whole place was built. I thought I knew the stones in the fireplace, where they came from and how they were laid. Oh.. and I know there's a safety shelter under the floor in case the Comanche attack, below the kitchen."

"Well, yes there is. How strange. My cousin Charlie found it when we were little. We used it when we played hide and seek with the other cousins. There were a lot of us then. But nobody ever found us there, even the big kids. It's a cave in the limestone; it opens from a place in the yard just off the kitchen. There's a door at the back of the root cellar. It's still there if you want to look when you're feeling better. I thought about turning it into a bomb shelter in the fifties but decided the whole thing was silly. Who would want to survive a nuclear war? Well, that's interesting, certainly. So you were here when this house was built, in some form anyway. What do you make of that?"

Gray lay back into his pillows. "Can we talk about it later? I'm exhausted from just thinking about it. The drugs are working again and I think that I'm going to sleep."

Wagner smiled his wise old smile and stood up to leave. "Good dreams then, my friend. Sleep well."

He walked out on the porch and looked out across his property, down his beautiful hills to the river. He smiled at the bright day and his beautiful ranch and his luck, his incredible good fortune. Carlos and Manuel drove by in the jeep, waving their hats. He waved back smiling. They'd both been born on the place. Carlos had just graduated from college in the city with a BA in business. He was trying to decide what to do next. Wagner had paid for his school and had offered him a job with the company but he'd figured Carlos would probably want to try his wings, and he did. The boy had always had a strong sense of adventure. Manuel had decided not to go to college yet. He really loved the ranch and he liked working on it. Wagner had told him he could use his college fund later if he wanted, or use it to start his own business if it turned out that way. Manny was dating Carlos's sister Gabriela, and had been, a long time now. Life… he thought, and he smiled. He needed to go see Mitchell Harris in the morning.

Then the rest of the dream came back to him, the part he didn't tell Gray. It was an even more vivid memory. He couldn't get it out of his mind. They were riding in the jeep. The big guy, Gray's friend was driving and yelling melacamo! at the top of his voice, over and over. Suddenly, Wagner was driving the jeep and he was alone and one of the locals drove up along side of him in a safari car. The local was cursing and he had a pistol and he shot at Wagner and the jeep went off the road and suddenly he was waking up yelling from a dream of falling into a brilliant white light that was all the colors he'd ever seen and some he'd never seen swirling together and he was falling and falling and falling.

# 35

# REFLECTIONS IN THE RIVER

There was a little park on the river just to the south of the city. It was a county park with perfect lawns and quiet arbors with benches and wild flowers, nestling gently into the curves of the river. Annie had been going there to think since she first came to school here. Though Gray thought she was afraid of the river, the opposite was true. She loved it. It gave her peace and courage and strength. The river was the reason she'd decided to go to school here. What bothered her, for some reason, was going with Gray to the river. It was strange but she couldn't get herself past it. She had no idea why.

There was almost never anyone at the park and when there was they disappeared into the river's welcome and became only distant echoes of children laughing and the joyful shouts of competition or victory from the soccer fields. Annie's secret place was there. It was a bench under a huge old cottonwood tree above a waterfall, where the spillway from an old cedar mill rejoined the river. The mill was only ruins now, concrete platforms and thick, low pieces of the crumbling walls with great stems of rusty iron protruding from the cement floor. The surface of the water in the spillway was flat and completely still above the dam. It gave a flawless reflection of the sky and the great limbs of the cottonwood. The place was remote, distanced from the rest of the park by an oak grove and a bend of the river. The few times she had seen anyone there they were lovers finding a place to be alone. When that happened she left and, if she had time, waited for them to come back up the trail. If she told people about it they always cautioned her that it was dangerous for a woman to go anywhere that isolated alone. So she stopped telling anyone about it. She felt perfectly at ease there, from her first visit. It was more than her usual self-confidence. She felt protected there, as if there were an invisible and impervious wall around the place. Today she was sad and fretful, thinking of Beth and envisioning her safe return from her kidnapping.

She sat on the park bench with her elbows on her knees and her head in her hands and stared at her reflection in the water. She never thought of herself as beautiful or even especially pretty, though everyone, male and female alike, said that she was both. She thought her face too strong, though her features were good, with a high forehead and a long straight nose. She thought her mouth looked harsh, even when she smiled. But she rarely ever thought of her appearance. Her focus was internal, where her music sang in the labyrinthine hallways of her mind.

As she watched her reflection, something strange seemed to happen. It was as if her face was moving toward her through the clear water. She blinked and shook her head but it changed nothing. Then her face emerged from the water below her and smiled up at her. It was an astounding feeling, unlike any she had ever known. For a moment she felt as if she were going crazy. Then she received a wave of love and warmth more encompassing than even her mother's love or Gray's. In front of her, emerging from the water, was herself, her naked, undisguised, smiling self. And though she didn't understand it in the least, she knew in that moment that she would never be the same again. Her life would never be the same again. "Hello Annie" she said and then she was sitting beside herself on the bench. Annie was having trouble with concepts. Her mind drifted in confused attempts at reason, dropping questions and words and guesses behind her, like debris down the swirling waters of a river in flood. Then, suddenly she was thinking in music and it all made sense, the divergent lines of a fugue coming together into a single, dominant whole. And it was over. She was alone on her bench again and the river swept away in a million glittering reflections of the light.

✳✳✳

Intermezzo III

*How strange, she thought. For a moment she was two, she and her human form. She wanted Annie to know that she had the right to power, that only the mortal dream separated them. And now Annie did know. It answered one question that had been with the naiad since her dream of Annie began. She and Annie could coexist in the same place without her avatar being reabsorbed by her presence. But she knew their oneness explained a lot to her human self and gave her power. Her experiment had worked perfectly. She could return to her song...*

# 36

## TWILIGHT

The sun had set in a buttermilk sky flushed in ranks of red gold. It reached out to an electric periwnkle blue to the north and south along the horizon. Now evening had dimmed to a faint remnant of rose and purple that would soon give way to darkness. It was warm in spite of the calendar and the old cedar rocking chairs moved in tandem as Gray and Annie held hands and tried to understand the path their lives had taken. They were listening to Beethoven's Ninth and sitting on the porch drinking a bottle of merlot. But even through the "Ode to Joy" they couldn't stop thinking about Beth. Annie had called Hank five times already today only to be told there was nothing to report. Hank was clearly losing his mind. He had given up trying to work and was driving the county hoping to find his wife by intuition or ESP alone. Gray was still shaky and looked awful but he said that he was feeling better. Annie hoped it wasn't just the drugs. They were going up to the main house for dinner with Wagner.

Annie went in and took a shower and Gray came in to wash her back and mess with her. It was his standard procedure. Normally she'd invite him in but she knew if she did that tonight that he would get carried away and though he was clearly better, he was probably not ready for "carried away". Besides, they would be late for dinner with Wagner. She sent him on his way, smiling wickedly when he groaned.

As she put on her makeup, she heard the phone ringing. She couldn't hear what Gray was saying but she knew that it wasn't good from the pitch of his voice. She was terrified that they had found Beth and she was badly hurt or something worse. Then Gray came to the bathroom door. His face looked stunned even behind his bandages.

Terrified she asked, "Honey, what is it?"

He tried, but couldn't speak for awhile. She could see that he was fighting back tears and she went to him and put her arms around him. "What… tell me… "

He gasped and said through a sob, "Wagner is dead." And for awhile he couldn't say anything else. They stood holding each other and crying until they regained control and she could ask what had happened.

"He was shot, about two, out on the highway near the cross-roads. There were several witnesses. Evidently he was driving toward the ranch and a small black car passed him and the driver shot him as he went by. He was hit once in the head and once in the neck. Then the truck ran off the road and crashed into a tree."

"Obviously it was Dewey," Annie shuddered. The whole world was crazy. "but why would he want to kill Wagner? He didn't even know Wagner."

"He knew Wagner and I were close and he did know him-from the fireworks stand. Wagner compared us both and chose me over him, just like you did. He probably knew that we were staying here too. And he's crazy. Who the hell knows what he's thinking or why?" Grey was having a very hard time with the guilt he was feeling...

Then he remembered that he still had to deal with things. "That was Mitchell on the phone. The county sheriff is sending a deputy to escort us to the courthouse. They're worried that Dewey might be waiting for us to come out and ambush us. We need to get ready."

At the courthouse they had to answer all the same questions about Dewey again. Mitchell Harris was there and also answered questions. The investigator asked if they were going to stay on the ranch. Gray said he didn't know where they would be, that he felt that without Wagner being there that they should probably go home. But he didn't know which one to go to. The sheriff suggested they go to Morningstar because they would be easier to protect there. He said he could have a car check the place all night long and access was limited to the low water bridge. When they said they would do that he recommended that they "keep their heads up and their eyes open."

On the way out Mitchell caught up with them and asked to talk to Gray a minute. He told him about how much Hans Wagner had appreciated knowing him and that part of it had to do with his mystical beliefs.

The lawyer said he didn't give much credence to that sort of thing but that Wagner was a very intelligent man and maybe, the lawyer said, he should reassess his position. "Whatever I think about his beliefs, Wagner clearly thought of you as a surrogate son, replacing the one he never sired himself. You know his wife died when they were young? She was killed in a car wreck. It was a real tragedy. He would never marry again. Anyway, I know you were fond of him as well. How could you not be? He was such a lovable old coot. At any rate, he was at my office rewriting his will this morning. It's finished and binding but I can't tell you what it says, by law, until the reading the day after tomorrow. But I suggest you come, 9 A.M.

Gray promised that he would be there and they drove out to Blue Heron Crossing with guarantees from the sheriff that he would have his deputy check on them through the night.

He was going home.

# 37

# WARNINGS

The buckskin snorted gratefully and grazed a patch of bright autumn wildflowers in the open meadow where Hans had dismounted. Ahead was a long valley where limestone hills swelled gently up from the river. Hans was enjoying a moment of peace. It had been a long, weary ride trailing Random's gang across the wilderness. He didn't think the outlaws knew that he was behind them, but they might, and that measure of doubt required constant caution. The tension was taking its toll. But here, from the crest of this rise, he could see in all directions and he could relax a little.

The trail showed that the gang had picked up several new members as they rode. They were still far from their former strength but his job was becoming more difficult as he went. He had to make his move soon, before any more outlaws joined the band.

Looking out across the quiet hills it occurred to him once again that this would be a fine place to live someday, after it had been quieted and calmed down some. Sometimes he tried to imagine what that future Texas would be like. It was possible for him to imagine peace, the Comanche gone, the outlaws in prison. It was more difficult to see his place in a future like that. He had become at home with violence and death. But hell, when he thought about it, the whole great country had. The Civil War had taught the entire male population death and murder as a way of life. And the women of the South and West had suffered through it too, while the women of the North had lived in fear for their men and the grief of losing them. Hatred and the call for vengeance came from the victors and the defeated alike. He doubted that the country would ever really heal. Move on, yes, but he thought it would twist the nation in ways no one could foresee. He remounted and started down the valley and into his grim vision of the future.

The day was alive with the signs of fall. He'd been seeing flights of geese and ducks, their bright v's escaping south to the coast and warmer climes, their lonely cries calling through the hills. Bright forest covered much of the valley. White oaks and Spanish oaks were showing their colors. The reds and oranges and yellows spilled through the dark green of the live oaks and cedars and the paler greens of the mesquite and sycamore. A few cypress trees and cottonwoods lined the river bank, flaming red-gold and rust. But, for the most part, the area of the river's course was bare limestone shelf rock, open below the bluff. The sun was still hot but a chill northwest wind cooled his face and promised a hard winter to follow the hard summer they'd just passed through. Texas, he thought. We should have gone to Illinois, Henry. I told you so. Henry didn't answer and Hans kept riding toward the river.

He saw a flash of reflected sunlight in a grove of trees ahead and to his right and he froze. He never doubted what he was seeing. It was death waiting for him, death, where the river skirted the foot of a round- topped hill a couple hundred feet higher than the river bank. Someone on that hill was waiting for him. He continued along the gully of a small creek, at the bottom of the rise, where the walls of the arroyo hid him from view. Then he urged his horse away from the river and up the creek. After dismounting he hobbled the buckskin and made his way on foot, heading toward the back of the slope, behind his waiting assassins.

Farley Wales and Merle Carlyle sat in a narrow limestone depression on the hill above the river. They thought themselves well hidden by the oak trees around them. Wales had taken off his sombrero and was combing his fingers through his sandy hair. In this hollow there was little breeze and he was sweating, even in the shade where he sat quietly waiting.

"Hey Merle, what river is that?" he asked. He was nervous and wanted to have something to think about besides the murder he had signed on for.

"Hell Farley, I don't know. There are maybe ten or more rivers across this mesa country. That could be any one of them. They all look the same." Carlyle was nervous too. He'd just been silently cussing the luck that brought him here and his own stupidity that had seen this bad idea as a way out.

His partner mirrored his misgivings. "Damn it, man, if we'd have just kept on heading west to Fredericksburg, we'd have found a ranch sooner or later. You ain't never shot nobody, nor me either. I don't want to be an outlaw. What the hell are we doing here anyway?"

"Well Farley, that's an easy one. You wanted to cut across country to Fredericksburg and when I said we should stick to the trail, you said we'd save time this way. So we got lost and wandered around in these stinking hills and the first people we saw were those outlaws. We were starving and they invited us to eat and then you got drunk with them and the next thing I knew we were part of the gang. Me, an outlaw. My ma would go crazy. I'm only sixteen."

Farley was older. He was twenty. Because he was senior, his vote always carried more weight. Merle was learning to regret that. The two had left Lufkin together over a year ago to join a cattle drive. They had both grown up ranching and never considered doing anything else. The cattle drive was going to be their great adventure. They were going to ride all the way to Dodge City, Kansas with a herd and then come back home, just the two of them on their own.

Farley got irate. "Well I don't remember you arguing for any other direction."

"Well, I'm arguing now. This is nuts. I say we head out before that fella' back there comes under our gun sights and we have to kill him. We just keep heading south and west until we hit Fredericksburg and then we work our way back home. And if we ever get there, I ain't never going nowheres else for the rest of my life. This adventure stinks." The longing in Merle's voice was plain as thunder.

"Great idea, son, except what do we tell that crazy-eyed son of a bitch who gave us these rifles when he catches up to us? That Random is the meanest-looking bastard I ever saw in my life. Remember what he said? 'I'll track you down and

kill you wherever you go.' Gave me chills the way he said it."
Farley stood up to look back down the river for their quarry.
"Speaking of that fella we're waiting for, where the hell did he
go? He was just coming around the foot of the hill."

The sound of a rifle bullet being chambered behind them
barely preceded the icy voice that echoed through their heads,
loud as church bells in the breathless morning air.

"All right gentlemen, drop all your weapons at your feet and
walk backwards five steps. And I mean all of them." Hans sounded
loud and terrifying to the two cowboys. It was the most terrifying sound either of them had ever heard. They never considered
resistance and the rifles were thrown down only seconds before
their pistols followed. Then they stepped slowly backwards.

"Good, my friends, very good. Now raise your hands above
your heads and turn around slowly." The boys did as they were
told. Hans looked them up and down.

"You" he said, pointing his rifle at Merle, "How old are you?"

"Sixteen, sir. Seventeen in December." Merle's voice was
shaking.

The rifle barrel swung to aim at Farley. "You?"

"Twenty, sir."

"So what in the hell are you two fellas doing in the bush-
whacking business? Why aren't you home doing chores for
your mamas where you belong?"

Farley took offense at being patronized. "We're drovers coming back from a cattle drive to Kansas. We been riding hard for over a year. Been through stampedes and blizzards and bar brawls and floods and we been lost and starving and nearly died of thirst... and we don't do chores unless we get paid for them." His temper was flaring. His partner kicked him to shut him up.

"Don't go getting all upset. But since you were hiding here waiting to kill me, I feel I have the right to take a few liberties. Especially since I have a Winchester rifle aimed at your chest." Hans almost smiled. He found himself liking these drovers in spite of himself. The older one reminded him a lot of Henry.

The question opened the floodgates and both cowboys started talking at once, explaining how they came to be in such a compromising situation. Hans eventually got the story sorted out and found himself sympathizing with them. He'd been listening earlier to their talk of Random and their precarious position before he'd interrupted their conversation with his rifle. But that didn't mean they wouldn't have killed him. He thought Random had sent them after him as much to get them out of his way as to murder Hans. The gang leader had to know these two had little chance of accomplishing that. Hans finally decided that, since they were new additions to the gang's roster, and hadn't been involved in Henry's murder, he didn't want to see them dead. Revenge and anger had cost him enough.

"So what should I do with you boys?" He mused aloud. "I ought to just kill you. That would be the smart thing to do.

Never leave an enemy alive to follow you. I learned that lesson a long time ago."

The drovers looked at each other nervously. Something in the older one's look made Hans swing his rifle back and forth between the two of them. "No, no boys. Don't go getting stupider. That would just relieve all doubt and I'd have to dig two graves. The thing is, I like you fellas and I'm sick of killing people. That bastard you're riding with sent you back here to die. I take offense at that. It may be that one or both of you will have to die fighting somebody sometime but it shouldn't be for that cold-blooded, snake-eyed son of a bitch. That's not right. I'm going to kill him anyway, but I'll include your names in my list of reasons."

Merle said "You think you'll kill him?"

Hans' look went hard as gun metal. "Oh yeah, I'll kill him. Only question is, will he kill me too." Then he realized what the cowboy was asking. "No son, he won't be coming after you if you ride away from here. His time has just about run out." Then he made up his mind. He left the two of them barefoot and tied to oak trees.

"Boys" he said, as he was leaving, "I didn't tie you up too tight. You'll be able to get free in awhile. Just be sure when you get to your horses that you mount up and get the hell out of here. Get your asses back to east Texas; and take my advice: stay there. If I see you following me I will kill you deader than old Stonewall Jackson."

They thanked him and swore they would go home and Merle, the younger one, apologized. Their boots and their guns and knives and horses he took down to the creek where he'd left his mount. Then he fired off their pistols and rifles in case anyone was listening. He left them there and rode on following their back trail to finish what he'd started.

*why do you ask us to leave the rivers
and the sun and the wind and live in houses?
Do not ask us to give up the buffalo for the sheep.
The young men have heard talk of this
and it has made them sad and angry.*

Chief Ten Bears

## COMANCHE

**M**ordecai was singing again. It wasn't that she didn't enjoy his singing. He had a wonderful voice, but he never stopped. He sang hymns and trail songs, even snatches of bawdy drinking songs from his youth that would have completely offended the ladies of his fellowship, but he only laughed when she expressed surprise. If he wasn't singing, he was reciting poetry or practicing a sermon. There were times when Sara wished that she could just be alone with her thoughts. She considered lagging behind out of earshot but the only time she tried it he stopped and waited for her to catch up. He told her that she needed to stay close where he could protect her. She couldn't say anything because she didn't want to chance hurting his feelings, so she just tried to think anyway. And sometimes she couldn't help but sing along.

It was, after all, a fine day for singing. It was blue sky perfect with the hills rolling away wrapped in autumn colors, the rust of the sycamores and the gold and red of the white oaks and Spanish oaks.

And every creek they passed was lined with cypresses and cottonwoods shading from bright gold to rust and floating the water in the creeks and carried by the currents down small waterfalls and rapids.

The few clouds were white silver and high and their drift was steadily north, marking the path for their earthbound followers. She hoped that they weren't building toward a stormy future somewhere ahead, and along the horizon a dark sky did seem to grow as they rode. This Hill Country of theirs was famous for its incredible thunderstorms and nearly instantaneous flash floods. There were many stories of people swept to their deaths by an unexpected surge of water coming down a normally dry creek bed from some storm far upstream. But when she mentioned the clouded horizon and her worries to the preacher, he began quoting scripture, as he always did.

"Deuteronomy, 31:6" he intoned dramatically. "Be strong and of good courage, fear not, nor be afraid…"

"Yes Mordecai" she said and smiled resignedly. They had developed a good relationship in the past few days. He knew that she was an unbeliever but felt that God had sent him to show her the way to the true path. She had to admit that his arrival as her rescuer after her desperate prayer had given her cause to wonder, but she had been raised on reason, not belief. She would not abandon it now.

The morning wore on into afternoon and they made good progress. This section of the trail was fairly civilized and there were stone bridges over the creeks in places. She wondered who built them. They looked old so she thought it might have been the Spanish when they first opened up the trail but she wondered if they even needed bridges that long ago. She wished that she knew more about Texas history and decided she would investigate if she had a chance to later. They were climbing a low hill coming up out of a small valley when Mordecai's horse whinnied. Charlemagne followed suit. Mordecai stopped short, and held his mount still, listening. Sara could hear nothing out of place.

"I think we might have trouble" he told Sara. "Let's kind of amble off the trail, sort of moving west, nice and slow like we're looking for a place to stop for lunch. Aim just off the trail, but keep moving toward the crest of the hill."

For the first time on the journey he took up the rear behind the Indian pony. The old horse had gone through a transformation since he left the lizard hanging kicking under the oak tree. He trotted along with new life, as if he'd gained back fifteen years. He was as energetic as the other horses and Mordecai used him as a pack horse. The preacher planned on taking him on to Menard with him and turning him loose on the high plains where White Tree had told him he'd found his horse, or where the horse found White Tree. The medicine chief had been off on a vision quest, trying to gain strong medicine and he had wandered without bearings. He found a young mustang waiting for him out on the plains. It never shied from him but waited patiently until White Tree reached him and mounted. Then the horse took him to water, and to his village.

That was why he died to protect his horse. The horse was his medicine.

Sara rode as naturally as she could with her heart pounding and her breathing coming fast. They were past the crest of the hill and a good distance west of the trail. Another valley stretched away in front of them looking peaceful and beautiful in its autumn colors. Near the crest of the hill there was a large limestone rock formation. A group of five Comanche warriors came from behind the rock shrieking, riding hard and firing rifles.

Sara pulled her rifle from its scabbard and Mordecai yelled at her to ride instead. "Head toward that arroyo where you see all those cottonwoods and cypress trees. That's the river. Ride hard and see what that big bay can do."

Sara dug her heels into Charlemagne's flanks and slapped his neck with the reins and urged him on. He responded like he'd been shot out of a cannon. Mordecai had dropped the lead rope for the Indian mustang and turned his horse to face the charging warriors. Sara realized that he was no longer beside her by the change in the noise level. She looked behind her and saw that the circuit rider was facing their attackers alone. He was probably fifty yards away and fifty yards from the Comanche and he was firing his pistols. The Indians were coming fast and firing their rifles or pistols as they came. Mordecai was shooting with both hands. Suddenly she was riding back toward the Comanche. She had her revolver in her hand and she fired as she came. Her first shot was wild. Her second shot was wild but lucky. She was alongside the preacher now. She had a terrible taste at the back of her throat and her ears were ringing from the roar of the gunfire. But all of it happened in slow motion. She saw every detail of the death of a warrior hit by Mordecai's bullets. He was hit twice in only a few seconds, both in the upper chest. The face went from battle rage, to surprise, to pain as he slipped from his horse and fell lifeless to the ground. Suddenly the battle roar was drowned out by the roar of the preacher's shot gun. He had slipped his side arms back in their holsters and raised the weapon he had been holding across his lap, a big double barreled twelve gauge that he called "Salvation". Now she understood why. The Comanche closest to them was carried backwards off his horse and lay sprawled in the buffalo grass. The two attackers who remained turned and fled.

Mordecai dismounted and sank to his knees beside his horse. She thought he was praying, thanking God for their deliverance. She joined him in the grass, out of respect, not belief. She knelt facing him, and only then did she realize that he'd been wounded. He was white as a ghost. His eyes were closed and his great, usually peaceful, face was locked in a grimace of pain. Blood streamed down his left side soaking his coat and staining the grass beneath him.

# 39

# FREDERICKSBURG

They got into Fredericksburg in the middle of the night. They rode through the night, pressing on against exhaustion, trying to get the preacher to the doctor before they lost him.

Sara had been trying to decide how to get Mordecai help, when a freight wagon came by driven by Mr. Friendly, the old driver who made runs from San Antonio to Menard and back every few weeks. There was a young cowboy on the bench beside him who was still cussing the horse that threw him and took off for parts unknown with everything he owned. He'd been walking for half a day in the direction his horse had gone and Friendly gave him a ride.

Between Sara and the old driver and the cowboy, they managed to lift the wounded man into the back of the wagon, and settle him as comfortably as they could. Even with three of them it took all the energy they could come up with to lift him. They used all the bedrolls and extra saddle blankets they had to cushion him against the rough wagon ride but it did little good. The road was rough and the wagon had only wooden slats for springs and even going slowly it was constantly jarring the preacher. Sara had managed to staunch the blood flow but was worried that the wound would open again and she would lose him. He'd lost a lot of blood already. So she held his head and shoulders on her lap and kept steady pressure on his wounds.

In Luckenbach, so small that it seemed barely a town at all, they sent for the new minister that Mordecai was supposed to meet. He came out from the trading post where he'd been awaiting his superior's arrival. The minister took one look at Mordecai's wounds and decided to get his buggy and drive him the ten miles to Fredericksburg. The buggy had springs and a much smoother ride and cushioned seats. The folks at the store brought out a mattress they kept for stray travelers, further softening Mordecai's ride. It became obvious that the minister was not only important, he was loved. By the time they got back on the road to the doctor in Fredericksburg, everyone for miles around had shown up. An escort of four men armed with rifles and pistols rode along with them, upset by the trouble with the Comanche.

"There ain't supposed to be any more Indians around here. General Mackenzie is supposed to have them all penned up on the reservation in the Territory" one of the riders said.

"Yeah, well, he did." Another man was riding beside the first. "Then they sent him to clean up the mess Custer made with the Cheyenne and Sioux. I knew we were gonna have trouble if he left. He's the only son of a bitch those fools ever found that…" Suddenly he realized that Sara was in the carriage beside him listening, and he stopped. "I beg your pardon ma'am. I'd forgotten you were there." She assured him that she forgave him and in a minute the two men had moved out of earshot.

Axel Schreiber was the town physician. He was a small intense man who moved quickly and made his decisions in a moment. The only hospital in town was a small clinic at his office. It had three beds where the physician would sometimes keep seriously ill patients close at hand if he had too many to travel to. There was a woman there who was having a difficult delivery and her husband had brought her in to find the doctor. Usually the midwives took care of the deliveries but for some reason she didn't have one.

When he saw Mordecai, the doctor became very upset. He told them that Brother Yell was his pastor and his good friend. He said they had dinner together whenever he came to town. He had the men, all of whom had crowded into the clinic, move a bed into his personal study and move his desk against the wall. Then he had them bring the circuit rider there. "The woman is going to be very noisy tonight, I think. He needs rest." Then, rather discourteously Sara thought, he threw them out. But Sara stayed, watching worriedly from across the crowded, book-lined office. The doctor hurried back and forth between his two patients, seemingly unaffected by his efforts or the lateness of the hour.

Mordecai's wound was on his left side, below his heart. The doctor said the bullet had gone in, ricocheted off two ribs, breaking them in the process, and gone back out to lodge in the bone of his left upper arm. The wounds were not terribly serious. The main problem was the blood loss. Before lodging in the bone of the upper arm it clipped the main artery. It hadn't severed it but it had done damage enough. He was going to operate and remove the bullet if possible and repair the damage. If it wasn't too extensive, he didn't think Mordecai would lose the arm.

He sent for Hugo Roth, the bartender at the Bluebonnet Saloon down the street. Roth had been a field hospital orderly during the War. Dr. Schreiber usually called him in to help if he had surgery. He also sent for his favorite midwife. He said it might be a long night for everybody.

The sun was high when Sara finally checked into the hotel to get some sleep. Mordecai was fine. The doctor said in two weeks he would be causing trouble and chasing off the Devil just like always. She was incredibly relieved. She'd been feeling guilty because the preacher stopped and waited for the Comanche, to protect her and gave her time to reach safety. He'd done more for her than anyone in her life before him. His loss would have devastated her. But, since he couldn't travel for a while she had to decide what to do without him. She had thought to ride with him all the way to Mason. Now it seemed, she was on her own again. She couldn't wait two weeks. She was going to press on one way or another.

But when she told herself that, she began to doubt the wisdom of the entire journey. She had been raped by a monster who would have eventually murdered her. She had been attacked by Comanche and might have wound up scalped and raped and tortured. Mordecai Yell had saved her twice. Without him she wondered how long she would survive. She had her girls to think of, and the child she carried. Perhaps it was time she came to her senses and went back to New Braunfels. She lay in the semi-dark of the hotel room and worried, until exhaustion swallowed everything.

It was mid morning the next day before she awakened, and she was ravenous. She went down to the dining room. Breakfast had already been served but the manager had heard her story. She went into the kitchen and made Sara's breakfast herself.

The tables in the dining room had white linen table cloths, and real silverware and crystal glassware. It was beautiful, elegant. The food was very good, with fine German coffee, sweet, the way she liked it. It made her very lonely for her mother. She wanted badly to be sitting in the dining room with her watching the morning grow brighter and listening to Beth and Annie playing on the porch. The manager came in and cleared her dishes away and brought back a pot of coffee. Beth asked her to sit with her a little and the woman smiled and went to get herself a cup. She said her name was Agnes and the hotel was owned by her uncle.

After introductions and Sara's thanks for the special service she'd been given, the woman proceeded to tell her about the twin boys that Meg O'Bryan had at Dr. Schreiber's clinic after Sara had collapsed. She marveled that it was her second set of twins, all boys.

"I don't know how that poor family can make ends meet. She's such a sweet and beautiful woman, hard working too. But her husband hasn't had much luck with the farm. Well, with the drought and everything, nobody around here has. He's Irish but he's no drunk. He's a good sober Presbyterian. He's a good carpenter too, but there's not a lot of that going on around here either. And they're proud. They won't take help.

That's why they had no midwife. They couldn't afford one. Now mind you, the midwives, we have two of them, they won't charge much, or not at all, but Danny, that's her husband, he considers it charity and he won't take it. Still, I bet they'll make it work somehow…"

She rattled on until Sara wondered why she had asked her to join her. She gave no entrance for replies or questions. Still her heart seemed kind enough and Sara couldn't help liking her. She was grateful when the bell sounded at the front desk and Agnes had to leave. A moment later a man stood at the door to the dining room, calling her name. It was Rob Enders, one of their closest neighbors in Mason.

"Sara! Dear Sara. What in heaven are you doing here? Jean will be so relieved. What has happened to you? You look exhausted. Have you sent word to your parents?"… and a dozen more questions, all coming so fast that she had no time to answer any of them. He put his hands on her shoulders as if to make sure she was real and he searched her face with his eyes. Finally he slowed down and sat beside her, holding her hand and drinking coffee, as if he were afraid she'd disappear if he let go.

He told her that her father had come to Mason several days before, searching for her. He told them that she'd ridden off alone seeking Hans. Half the community was out looking for her, or for Hans, to tell him about it. They were all afraid for her safety. Everyone would be so happy to know that she was all right.

Sara skipped the answers to his questions and started on her own. Had he heard back from Hans? What was he doing now? Did they know where he was? Enders said that so far as he knew no one knew where Hans was now. He told her about the ambush and that Hans had left, riding east, following the trail of the outlaws who'd escaped. He said Hans wouldn't listen to anyone. The other men with him came back. They told him to wait until they could regroup and form another posse. But he was afraid the trail would go cold and ignored their advice. He told her that Hans had been after the gang alone when they found him, waiting in ambush. He asked if he were despondent because she left, or for some other reason, because he seemed to be seeking death.

Sara told him about Hans's promise to help her with the ranch and forego his revenge, and that when they'd given up to the drought, he had told her in a letter that he was going to execute all of Henry's murderers. That was why she had taken off on her search. She offered no deeper explanation for either of their actions. When she told about her journey, she mentioned only that she'd met Mordecai Yell on the road and that he had offered her protection on her ride to Mason, if she would give him time to hold his services at his various congregations. She told him about the Comanche and Yell's wound and that the preacher was recovering. She said that she had decided to return to New Braunfels; which had been the truth until she spoke with Rob Enders. Now she realized that she couldn't give up on Hans until she found him. She lied and said that she was returning by stage for safety and would lead Charlemagne tied to the stage. She thanked Enders and asked him to tell everyone that she appreciated their efforts and concerns, but please tell them she was fine and would see them all soon.

Enders left her, seemingly satisfied, and began his ride back to Mason. Sara went up to her room and gathered her things.

She stopped at the dry goods store and added a few things to her gear, including an additional water bag and saddle bag and more bullets for both her pistol and rifle. She also bought a very wicked-looking knife with a scabbard that strapped on to her leg above her ankle where it was concealed by her boot. She picked up a new boys' outfit to wear and a new wide-brimmed hat and a compass. Then she walked down to the livery and paid them and had them saddle Charlemagne. She gave the boy there a half dollar to take a letter to Mordecai at the local Methodist preacher's house where he was staying until he healed. She wrote him that she would always be more grateful than he could ever know. She apologized for leaving this way but said that she had to return to her quest and knew that he would not approve. She promised to let him know when she was safe and would seek him out wherever he might be. Then she rode out of town heading northwest into the hills, because from what Rob Enders had told her, that was where Random and his crew were heading, with Hans trailing in their wake.

# 40

## RISING WATERS

They drove home without problems. Their grief filled them and overflowed. It started them crying time after time. Gray said that it made no sense; that Wagner would still be alive if he wasn't Gray's friend. "And I've known him less than a month. It's crazy. And now he's dead and I'm written into his will? I feel complicit."

"Don't be ridiculous." Annie said. "Wagner was no fool. He didn't act out of ignorance or insanity. I've never known a person with more personal wisdom… or intelligence. If his ideas sound crazy to you, maybe you should do what Mitchell said he was going to do. Maybe you should reevaluate them."

She drove on through the night, occasionally catching sight of the county sheriff's patrol car in her rearview mirror. There was a lot of lightning in the west and southwest but it was pretty far away.

Then she said, "Show me your watch."

Gray pulled it out of his pocket and looked at it.

"Open it." Annie said quietly. And the music of the old song filled Annie's car. He was glad that Annie was driving because he began to lose it again. Annie put her hand on his shoulder. "Would he have given you that without a solid reason, love? Would you give it to a stranger?" She let him think for awhile. Then she said "The last time Hans Wagner and I spoke, in depth, was yesterday when he drove me to meet Hank at my apartment after Beth was kidnapped. I told him that I was sorry for putting everyone in danger. Do you know what he told me? He said that I shouldn't worry about putting him in jeopardy. He said that he could live fearlessly because he knew that each of us, everyone, is protected by their personal destiny. He thought that nothing could prevent the end of his allotted time but that until it came nothing could stop him. He said he'd come through all sorts of really dangerous moments unhurt, and when the moment came for him to die, he was ready, whatever the reason. I think that you should believe him."

As they turned into the low water crossing, Annie watched the sheriff pull over and turn around, facing the road and covered in shadows back in some trees. She could see he had a clear view across the river to Gray's cottage. He could also watch the one lane bridge. She didn't know how long he would be there but she wished him luck in staying awake. They went into the Crossing ready to collapse but when they came through the door, Gray realized that he'd never cleaned up after Dewey shot out the windows. There hadn't been time. He'd done the basics, but he hadn't had time to deal with the main damage, the bullet holes and structural repairs. It was a shock to see it again. He decided to put off thinking about how to fix it all until some better day, and he and Annie went to bed.

They woke together to the sound of thunder rolling and rolling. The windows rattled. Lightning flashes cast flickering shadows across the bedroom. The Georgia cane at the window was rattling and sighing and tossing. Then the rain came on the Crossing's corrugated metal roof. The first drops were loud and slow and heavy. Then the storm arrived in earnest, fast and hard. Annie burrowed her head into Gray's shoulder and sighed... "The rain, darling, the rain..." He wrapped his arms around her and stroked her hair. Occasional lightning flashes disturbed the somber twilight of the bedroom. The rain on the metal roof was coming down so hard that it drowned out the sound of the thunder. Strange things happen to time while rainstorms rule the world. Clocks seem useless. Everything is limited to the rush of wind and the drum of falling water and the occasional punctuations of lightning and thunder. And somehow that changes the texture of life entirely. They slipped back into the shadows of their dreams and lost track of the rainy world.

Gray woke from sleep, still in the full dark, at some urgent prompting from his dreams. He felt a sense of foreboding that refused even his exhausted refusal. His nerves were raw, and he tried to figure out what had awakened him. Finally he went to the window. In the lightning he could see that the county sheriff's car was gone from the dam. He also saw why. The river was raging. The low water crossing was obviously closed by the flood. The water was topping the banks below the dam and the roar of the water was terrifying. He had seen this twice before. The little yellow house on the bluff had never flooded, although a couple of times the water had come almost to the crest- but not quite, never. It always stopped just at the upper end of the drive, and the Crossing itself stayed dry. Alonzo said that even in the 1955 flood, the one hundred year flood that killed twenty-two people, it came right up to the threshold and stopped, like a Jehovah's Witness who needed to be invited in. But Gray wondered about this one. He had never seen rain like this. Since he last looked out the window it had grown in intensity. He could no longer see to the other side of the river. The rain was too heavy.

He woke Annie. "Listen love, you need to wake up; can you? Come on darlin'. Wake up now…" and so she rose and made the coffee and kept him company during his adrenaline-fed vigil. It was no great comfort for him to know that for the entire length of the river and up every tributary creek anxious people were keeping the same watch. Only the passing of the rainstorm would lessen their fears. He was worried about going on the internet to get a weather report because it was often hailed as the perfect bait to lure a thunderbolt. Finally, Gray was worried enough to risk it. Sure enough, the storm stretched all the way to the Gulf and appeared to have the same intensity all the way. The report said it could go on like this for two days. They had already gotten over six inches of rain in some areas of the Hill Country. That might be disastrous. Sometimes rain to the west would cause flooding before anyone in Morning Star ever saw a drop. They already had flash flood alerts on all over the Hill Country. They had already closed some highways and all the low water crossings. There were the usual warnings that everyone should be extremely careful about low-lying areas." Do not chance being swept away. Every year people gamble and lose." Gray decided it was time to leave.

They packed up all that they could reasonably carry. They loaded their computers and instruments and special pictures and books, a couple changes of clothes for Gray. Most of

Annie's things were still in her apartment. It wasn't supposed to flood in the city anymore. They'd built all sorts of flood control dams to protect the neighborhoods. Still, you never knew how a flood was going to go.

There was a farm road to use for the few houses in the area across the river, a back way out when the low water crossing was closed. It was all caliche or dirt roads and in rainy seasons it was hard to get through sometimes, because it could get muddy, but tonight they had no choice. Gray drove because Annie had never used the exit before. It wound through three different ranches and came out on another county road five miles away but it never crossed the river.

They had gone through several stock gates that were open when they were usually closed. Then they came around a corner in the dark and there were a bunch of drovers on horseback herding cattle. It was like a scene from the nineteenth century, or some movie about the Chisholm Trail. The herd stretched off into the rain and darkness and it was impossible to see how far it went. It was clearly a big herd. The cowboys were wearing yellow rain gear and they had plastic liners on their hats. They were all waving flashlights and lassos and they were yelling at the cattle to keep them moving. They yelled "yup, yup" and "Get along now", or whup, whup, whup", just noises, herding them down the road and into another pasture. Two of the cowboys rode over to the car and Gray saw that it was Alonzo and Mr. Anderson, who owned the largest of the adjacent ranches.

"Where you kids headed?" Anderson asked after they'd all said hello. The rain was drenching the world like Noah's flood. Annie couldn't understand how the men stayed in their saddles.

Gray told them they were getting out because they had to work tomorrow and they didn't want to get stuck out here and miss the hours. He told them they were getting nervous about flooding as well. He asked what was going on with the cattle.

"We're moving them to the highest pasture we got around here son. You want to help? You know I always have a horse for you Gray." Alonzo was smiling at his joke. Anderson was too. "Besides" he continued, "I think you've already missed the boat on that escape route. I think Mitchell Creek is probably under water."

Gray was puzzled. "But it's not that low. It's hardly a trickle. Most of the time it's bone dry, even when the bridge is closed."

"You're right." Anderson said. "But son, this ain't most of the time. Weatherman is saying it could be a five hundred year flood. Nobody round here's ever seen a five hundred year flood. If it gets that bad you're gonna lose your place. Hell, 'Lonzo might even lose his, and it's got a good bit higher elevation than yours. And Mitchell Creek might be a Niagara Falls by now. Ya'll best come stay at my place 'til this is over. Helen would love to have visitors."

Gray asked if anyone had been down to see if this road was still open.

"Nope. We've had our hands full, you might say. We had a lot of beef to bring in." Anderson was clearly worried about them. "Look Gray, don't take chances. Everyone who bucks the odds in weather like this winds up sorry."

Gray thanked them both and said they were just going to look at the creek and if it was flooded they'd come back and take them up on their hospitality. The two men waved at them, still shaking their heads, and went back to work.

The road was the worst he'd ever seen it. The muddy places were almost impassable, but Gray brought the little car through by driving with two wheels on the high side of the road. It was very hard to see. He was having a hard time identifying where he was on the road. He hadn't had to use it that much, never more than a few times a year, and in this downpour visibility only occurred in spurts with the bright lightning flashes. He was negotiating a sharp turn along a stock fence when a bright flash of lightning showed a downhill path ahead. There was a large muddy spot at the corner so he speeded up to get through it and then they were floating. It happened so quickly. He threw the car in reverse and felt the wheels start to catch. The back of the car pulled to the right throwing the front to the left and he was about to feel relieved when the back tire lost its grip and they were floating again. The current was extremely fast. He started to yell- Get out! Jump out! And then it was too late. They were being swept like a leaf down a raging river. Only it wasn't a river. It was Mitchell Creek and should have been no problem at all. This was clearly not a normal flood. The water was half way up the windows and the car was acting like a raft. It didn't seem to be sinking.

Annie said "So what's next?"

The water was almost to the top of the windows and then they couldn't see. The headlights were gone.

Annie took his hand and said "I love you." But she sounded remarkably calm. He told her that he was so glad he had found her and that he loved her with all his heart. He wasn't afraid. He wondered why, but he felt no fear. He kept thinking of things to try to fight back against the river and death but he couldn't think of anything that he thought would work. Strangely, the car was still floating. The current was so strong it was carrying them down the flood like a fishing cork.

"This voyage shouldn't last long" he thought, but it did. The car actually seemed to be becoming more buoyant and riding higher. Then he heard her song, the river woman's. He decided he was going crazy. The roar of the waters and thunder and wind should have drowned out everything else. He could barely hear Annie's voice beside him on the seat but that same melody that he had searched for all those evenings, full of longing and mystery, was rising through the din of the flood, and Annie, Annie was singing along. It grew louder as they went until the elements of the storm were like instruments in a symphony. They all came together playing an indescribable melody, only Annie was harmonizing.

He didn't know what he'd expected but it wasn't this. They were riding above the flood, as if the chassis was watertight. Through the windows the constant lightning revealed that they were in the river now and riding high. Then he noticed that the interior of the car was still dry. His feet weren't even wet. Suddenly the front wheels hit something and the car lurched and they were rolling on land. He looked out the window and saw tombstones revealed in a flash of lightning and he opened the door and stepped out into the downpour. He was standing in the Morningstar cemetery, just across the river and upstream from the Crossing.

He yelled to Annie to get out of the car and then realized that she was standing beside him with an open umbrella and her arm around his waist. He felt stunned. His mind wouldn't grasp what had happened. He wondered if he was dreaming or hallucinating in death. It made no sense. He held Annie a moment until she said "Let's get out of the rain." He was afraid to get back in the car, in case the river was still rising, though it was fifty feet or more from the water line. He led her to the front entrance of the old mill where he'd gone many times exploring. There was a way that you could force the front door without breaking it. A twelve year old boy showed it to him the first time he explored the ruins. He'd seen Gray peering in the windows and told him he'd show him how to get in if Gray gave him a dollar. It was a dollar well spent. Six years later he and Annie were standing in the big gloomy entrance looking out through a very dirty window at the rain. It was cold but they were alive and safe.

# 41

## THE TRAIL OF THE HEART

**S**he was on the wide prairie shortly after waking. The day's first light swelled to the lonely sigh of wind through the deep grass. Great slow hills rolled out towards the east and a fierce and fiery sky. She had spent a night much like the first of the journey. This time though, she stopped earlier in the evening so she'd been able to pick a more comfortable setting in a small clearing well hidden from view. She'd even eaten breakfast, though it was only biscuits and water. Charlemagne had oats and drank a little from her Stetson, which she had taken the time to beat up until it looked old and weathered. Amazing the damage you could do to a hat with trail dust, water and boot prints.

She had no idea where she was going or where to find Hans. She wasn't sure she could even find water or avoid trouble once she got into the wilder country. It would have been easier on the Pinto Trail but according to what she heard from Enders, Hans wasn't on the trail. He was out in the nameless open wilderness and she had only her luck and her heart to guide her. She asked the owner of the stable if there were any towns north of Fredericksburg.

"Well, there's a little cow town called Llano northeast about thirty or forty miles. Ain't got much to recommend it but some messed up mud streets and a tavern. But north? North there ain't nothing' but scrub oak, cedar and hard times."

As she called upon her resolve, and courage, and love, and rode into the wilderness, she thought back to Mordecai singing "The Linden Tree" with Gertie in Sisterdale and she began to sing. "At wellside by the ramparts, there stands a linden tree…"

The wilderness was almost completely empty of anything suggesting the arrival of human kind from their earlier haunts across the oceans. To Sara's north the scrub oak and cedar grew gradually thinner until they disappeared entirely and only the grass remained, stretching away north and west, wave upon wave like a great green and yellow sea. The immense emptiness was not really empty. Life surged and struggled in uncountable forms and numbers. The great buffalo herds were almost gone, wiped out in the campaign to destroy the plains tribes, but white tail deer and antelope still ranged. And they were still attended by the hunters, wolves and coyotes and black bear. More exotic species also roamed the area, ocelots and javalinas. Even an occasional jaguar traveled north to prey on the great bounty of the herds. Many other species still teemed and would continue the struggle for many years to come; until the ranchers and the farmers wiped them out as well. Some of the smaller creatures, being beneath the attention of the new clans, would continue in the struggle for life by virtue of their adaptability. But the farmers and the ranchers hadn't arrived yet. The emptiness was now largely undisturbed except by occasional bands of young Comanche and Kiowa warriors, unblooded and trying desperately to pursue the old ways, escaping to freedom from stifling reservations. But she was already familiar with them. There were also small bands of outlaws hiding out in the vastness to escape past mistakes or present retribution from the civilized world further east. She knew about them as well.

Riley Cope and Charlie Anders were riding east in a sullen mood. Anders was nearly snarling. "What I don't get is why I get this shit detail with you. I know Random's pissed at you because you should have killed that fucking German when you had the chance. Instead you just let him kill McReady and you ran like a deer. Hell, now the son of a bitch is still chasing us and aiming to kill us all."

"Look, you jackass, if Random is pissed it's 'cause he's scared himself." Cope was nearly yelling. "You don't see him going back after the German. Hell no. He sends those two new guys, and so of course they get themselves killed. They weren't even professionals, just a couple of down on their luck drovers looking for a quick score. What did he expect? The German's crazy but he's good. And maybe more. I mean, you were there. We combed that whole canyon. Cooper swore he got him and Cooper was good. So, what I want to know is, where the hell was he? And how come he was shooting McReady the very next day? There's something weird going on there."

Charlie Anders yelled back. "You're crazy. And you're stupid if you think Random's afraid of anything. That son of a bitch is ice cold. He don't get scared. I seen him pull some things would make you piss your pants. Besides, we don't know that the German killed them. I think they missed him and the minute he fired back they took off for St. Louis as fast as their broke down ponies could travel. Nobody ever went back to check. All we just know is we heard the rifles and they never come back. Anyway, if Weasel ever gets here he'll get rid of the bastard soon enough. That one is invincible."

"If he is" Cope sneered, "it's because the way he smells has any normal person tossing their dinner when he gets close enough to shoot. And you're his pal. That's why you got sent to fetch him. I'm just here to protect you." He sniffed the air loudly. "Just how close are you two anyway? I think you're starting to smell like him."

"I ought to kill you, you son of a bitch." Anders growled.

Cope turned his horse and sat facing him, his hand above his pistol. "Whenever you think you're man enough, you just go ahead. You ain't Random and you ain't your buddy the Weasel. I'll put so many holes in you, you'll leak like a rusty bucket."

Ander's eyes got wide and a look of fear crossed his face. He spoke again in a friendlier tone. "Listen I didn't mean to get you all riled up. We got to stick together. Once we get to Nacogdoches we'll be back in the money. I'll bet Random has all kinds of jobs lined up. I think we should have just left this damn country when things started going bad, back when we jumped those German's in the first place."

Cope relaxed."You're probably right. But Cooper wasn't leaving. I think Random thought he was worth sticking around for. And them ranchers were paying good money." Then his voice went thick with sarcasm. "So, this is your job, boss. The Weasel wasn't at the meeting spot. How far do you plan on going to find him?"

Ander's took off his hat and wiped the sweat from his forehead with a bandana. "Hell, I don't know. We don't even know which way he was gonna take. This whole damn trip is a waste of time. I am sick of riding and if I ever get shed of this crew I am going back to St. Louis and I never want to mount another horse as long as I live. I'll get me an honest job and live out my days in peace."

Cope started laughing. "Oh yeah, I can just see that. An honest job? You wouldn't know honest if it walked up to you and shook hands."

Anders acted offended. "Well, that's a damned lie. Why I'd have you know that I try to do a little something honest every day." Then he spurred his mount and rode on ahead, laughing at his joke. Through the scrub oaks ahead he saw a rider coming. He went back to Cope signaling quiet.

He told him someone was coming their way and he looked too small to be the Weasel. "You move ahead to that gap in the cedars." He said. "I'll circle around behind him."

Sara was making her way from cedar brake to cedar brake trying to stay out of sight as much as possible. The trees had thinned out a lot so there was no way for her to remain constantly hidden. The long emptiness with no one's voice but her own for company had lulled her into a sleepy haze. She rode between the cedars and suddenly found her path blocked by a man on a horse with a rifle aimed at her chest. When she tried to turn Charlemagne to run, she faced another mounted man with a rifle. And she was captive again.

# 42

## HOSTAGE

When she was first captured she thought she was going to be raped again or murdered for her horse, and she probably would have been, except that one of the two men who held her captive recognized her immediately. He knew her from Mason, he said, and he knew that she was a woman. The other one knew she was a woman as well, and from the way he smiled at her, she felt things were going to go badly for her. She was thinking of the knife in her boot. They hadn't found that. But the one named Riley told him who she was and to back off.

"Charlie, this is Miller's woman." He said. "We finally got lucky."

She was amazed to learn that she had been captured by the same men Hans was tracking, the same men who had killed Henry. And then, somehow, she knew everything was going to be all right. It was too strange to be a coincidence, just too strange. She could feel fate working behind everything that had happened and she knew in her heart it would all work out in the end. She was also shocked to hear herself called "Miller's woman". It gave her new insight about how her year with Hans had been viewed by the town. And, strangely, it brought her a feeling of happiness, down underneath everything else.

The one named Riley, who took off his hat and called her ma'am when he spoke to her, told her that it would be all right. He told her they would trade her to Hans and Hans would leave them alone. He'd already had his pound of flesh, after all, he said and she was surely more important to their enemy than vengeance. She supposed or hoped that that was true. The other man wasn't happy about that. He grabbed Riley and pulled him aside. She couldn't hear what he said but she heard what Riley said. "For Christ sake, do you think, if we hurt her, that Miller would ever stop hunting us? It would get even worse. He'd be even crazier."

In the end Charlie saw reason, though it only seemed to be final when Riley said they should let Random decide. Then she knew that they weren't the only outlaws left and that nothing was finished yet. She was surprised to learn from their conversation as they rode that these were the same men the lizard had been on his way to meet. She didn't share that information however. But it gave her chills to remember what her tormentor had described to her constantly when she'd been his prisoner, about how he and his friends would share her when they all got together.

The outlaws' camp was beside a sunny river bank under the shade of some huge old cypress trees. It seemed incongruous somehow that this peaceful setting could hold so much cruelty and hurtfulness.

Five men sat in various places around a campfire. When her captors presented her to their leader he wouldn't believe them about who she was at first. But another man said that Riley was right. He'd seen her with Hans many times.

Random got pissed "If you two saw the German so many times why didn't you kill him?"

Riley started backing up right away. She could see that he was afraid of the leader. "Well hell Random, I was alone and I wasn't going to take him on by myself. I only saw them twice. I went looking for you both times but you and the boys weren't around."

"Ah, you know what's wrong with you Cope? You need to grow some cojones. You're just a little girl in a man's body. If I wasn't so short-handed right now I'd shoot your ass myself and leave your bones for the buzzards."

Then the leader turned on Sara's other witness. The man had been wounded. His shirt was bloody and he was pale as the sun-bleached limestone that he was leaning against. "And you Whiskey, when did you turn chicken shit yellow? I always thought I could count on you."

The wounded man looked at Random as if he was trying to bring him into focus. "Well boss, I figured I'd see him when we were all there and could take him easy. He wasn't hiding. I didn't think he could do that much damage and I was waiting 'til the time was right. You want to shoot me too, then go ahead. I can already tell I'm never leaving this crossing." His voice came out breathless and he stopped talking half way through and then started again. He did look like he was dying. Sara found herself feeling sorry for him and made herself stop.

He was a murderer and a bully and he was dying as he'd lived. She could hear Mordecai speaking from her memory.

The chief turned to Charlie, her disappointed captor. "So where's Weasel?" he asked quietly.

"He never showed up, Random. We waited half a day and then we went looking for him. We were searching for signs of him when we found her. And when Cope recognized her I thought we should bring her to you right away" Anders lied. Cope said nothing. He was keeping as quiet as he could, trying to manage the trick of invisibility.

"Well, you were right. Did you mess with her? She ain't bad looking." Random looked at her like she was a horse he thought about buying.

"No sir. I thought we might want to keep her undamaged in case you wanted to trade for her." She could see the devious soul behind Anders' ingratiating smile. It was an interesting character study. Cope got up and left the clearing.

"Well. I'm surprised. But good thinking just the same. And you're right. The son of a bitch would probably spend every minute of the rest of his life hunting us down. Course he probably will anyway 'cause I think he's more interested in us killing him than he is in killing us. Doesn't help us though; just makes him more dangerous. Let's just try to help him get what he wants. Anyway, I wonder where the old Weasel got off to. I doubt anyone finally got him, but you never know. Tell you the truth, I'm glad. The guy's a real live monster. I never liked seeing him coming. Part of it's just his smell. Christ, he smells like a corpse the coyotes dug up."

Cope came back to the fire clearly excited. "I think Miller is out there. I heard a horse whinny a good ways off."

Random said, "Well that would be about right. I think he was a half a day behind us." Then he walked to the edge of the clearing and shouted "Hey Miller, that you out there?" A rifle shot echoed through the trees and the bullet whined past and hit a big cypress behind Random across the clearing.

"Now hold on a minute. We got somebody you might want to talk to. By the strangest twist of fate, your sweetheart is here with us" he turned his head and spoke to Sara over his shoulder. "What's your name lady?"

Sara looked at him coldly. Random said "Go on, say something to him." She refused to answer him. He moved across to Sara and grabbed her arm and roughly pulled her to the center of the clearing. "Well, seems she don't want to talk to you, but I guess you can see her all right. Recognize her?" He pulled Sara's hat off and tossed it aside. "She's blonde, blue-eyed, good looking… in a skinny kind of a way. The thing is, it's too bad for her if she ain't your sweetheart 'cause she's gonna start taking off her clothes to give you additional reminders and if you still ain't recognized her by the time she's stripped, then I'm just gonna shoot her, or give her to the boys to finish. What do you think?" Random's voice echoed off the banks of the river upstream from the crossing.

Sara had had enough. She jerked her arm loose from the outlaw's grasp and ran for the river. She made it almost to the other side before Anders caught her.

Cope and the others stopped at the river bank. They were all in pursuit as well. Sara continued fighting Anders' attempt to bring her back and a couple of the others went to help him.

Hans walked out of the cedars and stood at the edge of the clearing with a pistol in each hand. Then he spoke. "All right, leave her alone. I'm here."

"Well so you are. And if you'll just toss those pistols over here I'll have the fellas set her free." Random sounded mockingly light-hearted.

Hans let the hammers down on his weapons and tossed them across to Random's feet.

Random said "Good deal. Now come on over here and join us."

Hans walked across the clearing and stood at the edge of the group. Sara was still in the river surrounded by Random's gang. She ran back past the outlaws again and was standing beside Hans before they realized she was gone. They were all watching Hans and Random.

Hans put his arm around her and, in spite of everything, Sara knew it was all right again.

Random was smiling mockingly. "Well that's sweet. Now, you know I'm going to have to kill you, right? If I don't you'll be right back after me, as soon as she's back home. You understand that right?"

Hans nodded. "Just let her go safely."

"Sure will. She's too skinny for me. Course, I could just keep her around a while and fatten her up a little…" Hans's eyes went hard as death and he reached out and grabbed for Random's pistol and then everything happened at once. Even years later, she was still trying to sort it all out in her mind.

The wind was suddenly screaming. The outlaws were all pulling their guns. Hans was shoving Random and Random was trying to get his gun up and a wall of water came down the river out of the limestone banks just upstream from the crossing and then they were yelling and then they were all gone. She thought she saw a beautiful naked woman there with her arms around Hans, for an instant only, and then she was gone and the water rushed past and the river was back in its banks and the only outlaw left was the wounded one, only he was dead, and then a blue heron flew past going downstream about shoulder high and Hans was holding her while she told him about Clara and the lizard and Mordecai Yell and there was music coming out of the air and the sun was filtering down through the branches of the cypresses and then there was only the river glittering in the noontime light while every cardinal in the world was singing all at once in the branches of the surrounding cedars.

# 43

# 1920

**H**ans sat in his cedar rocker watching the dawn grow brighter across the valley to the north. On clear mornings you could see the line of the river written in cypress trees a little over four miles away.

All of it was his ranch, his home. He and Henry had chosen this ridge for the view when they first started looking for land. When they claimed it you had to climb a big oak to see what the view was. Now after clearing a few hundred cedars you could see that they'd chosen well. Originally, this had been Henry's place- five hundred acres. Hans bought a nearly identical 500 acres farther west. A man named Albrecht owned the place in between but during the War, a Comanche raiding party had killed him and burned his cabin. Hans was fighting in Virginia at the time. Henry had written him to tell what happened. He said he'd seen the smoke and rode over as fast as he could. He found Albrecht scalped and hanging upside down from a sycamore tree. The War years were bad years for the pioneers.

After the Hoodoo passed and Hans and Sara married, they bought Albrecht's land and worked all three places. Hans still marveled at Sara's determination and skill. She was one of the first land owners to get into big time cotton production and it really paid off. In the 90's when everyone else was losing money and selling land because of the bad economy, Sara was making money and buying land. In '93 they bought a thousand acres from Anderson. It lay down the valley toward the river. Finally, they'd bought up the remaining land separating them from the water. Five thousand acres they owned and a little more. And that was just this place. She bought more land along the river, south of the escarpment, where the limestone gave way to black dirt and everything she planted flourished. Hans was amazed. He would never have done that on his own. Land was Sara's passion, the way she kept track of her success. And she wasn't hard in her dealings. Everyone loved her and everyone that she did business with went away happy. She had a knack of making good deals good for everyone.

The Reverend Mordecai Yell became a regular visitor to the house. After he'd recovered from his wounds enough to travel, he'd married them. They'd gone back to New Braunfels and were married in her parents' parlor with Annie and Beth as bridesmaids. Later, when Mordecai came to Mason on his journeys as Presiding Elder, he'd always stay two or three days. Once he brought his whole family to stay for a week. The kids were adolescents. The four Yell children and his and Sara's three girls had a great time together. Zeke, the Yells' youngest, became Bethie's first love. When he left she pined away for six months and wrote him dozens of letters. Sara really liked Peggy, Mordecai's wife. And Hans and Mordecai became fast friends. When they'd been married for two years, Sara informed him that she was going to be baptized and wanted them to become members of the Methodist congregation in Mason. He was surprised but he agreed to join and even went to services with her sometimes, but he was never baptized. He wasn't a believer and he refused to be a hypocrite. Mordecai never said a word about it. They were real friends.

In those years Hans had wanted to build a house on a bluff by the river. But Sara wouldn't have it. She remained jealous of Hans's "river woman", as she called her, all their married life. Sara died last year in the influenza epidemic. He still didn't understand her death. She was so strong. In all their years together he couldn't remember her being sick, ever. And he was old. He should have been the one who died. But he'd only had a slight fever and been fine and she was gone. Forty three years they'd been married. What an amazing woman she was.

Angie came scolding out of the house from the front room. The screen door slapped shut behind her. "Hans, you ate no breakfast. I made tortillas fresh for you. Good huevos just the way you like. Why don't you eat?" Angie was his cook and housekeeper and had been for thirty-plus years. Sara had taught her all her German recipes, but since Sara died, she usually cooked Mexican food because Hans liked it better. His eating habits were the cause of a longstanding argument. These days, once he got his coffee, he had all the breakfast he wanted. "I am old". He told himself, smiling. "That's all it is. I've outlived all my appetites."

Angie's husband Daniel was the last hired hand on the place. After Sara's death, Hans had lost interest in the ranch. He sold off the stock and let the fields go fallow. He had a few horses and two milk cows and some chickens, but that was it.

He'd leased out the land across the road to Anderson's boys. It seemed fitting, since he bought a lot of it from their father in the first place. Anderson had lost a herd on his last trail drive north. He'd run into fences and quarantines in Kansas. They said they had to keep Texas cattle out because they had the Texas fever and when he tried to move them back south the law impounded them. He went to court and got them released but in the end he still wound up losing his shirt. He had to sell off half his acreage to stay in business and he never tried a big drive again. Anderson had died in 1910. Hans missed their battles over stock and land and money. Hell, he just missed him. They were all gone, all his old enemies and friends. He was the last of his tribe.

Then it occurred to him again for the fifth or sixth time this morning that it was his birthday. He was eighty-five years old today. He groaned. All the kids were coming to the party... and half the town as well. Anderson's boys were barbecuing a whole steer. It was going to be a big night. Mariachis would play through dinner and after there would be a barn dance with Rawlings and his bunch. That would be good. He loved fiddle music. And Rawlings would accompany Hans when he picked up the guitar to play the "Linden Tree" like he always did at fiestas. It had always been Sara's favorite. He opened the pocket watch she gave him for their thirtieth anniversary. The crystalline music of its chimes played the old German folk melody that had always been her favorite. *"At wellside by the ramparts there stands a linden tree..."* He wondered if his voice could still manage to get through it. He and Daniel had planted a Linden tree at her grave on her last birthday. Had to drive half way to Bandera to find one. *"and still I hear it whispering. You'll find your peace with me."* Damn, how his mind wandered.

And the kids were all coming, Beth and Annie and Clara and Young Hans...Hans smiled. Young Hans was almost forty-one now... Hans was a great-grandfather many times over. Annie married one of the O'Bryan boys. They had four children, including twin sons. Clara had married the Mitchell boy, and her sweet daughter Sara had married the Wagner boy last spring and now she was expecting. He didn't have favorites but if he had, Sara would be his favorite. He would be a great-grandfather again. Young Hans had married one of the Mitchells too, Becky the youngest of Tom's six kids, but they hadn't made him a grandfather.

He also knew that his children were going to try to talk him into leaving the ranch and moving in with one of them. Every time he saw any of them these days it was the same worried discussion. Hell, he knew he was old. He understood. It was hell getting to sleep and it was hell waking up. It hurt to walk and it hurt to sit down and worst of all was standing back up. His strength was long gone and one day, probably soon, he'd be gone. This birthday would give their argument added weight- in their eyes. He was very lucky. He had wonderful children. Every one of them wanted him with them, or said they did anyway. So far though, his thinking was still clear and he wasn't going anywhere. He'd made up his mind about that.

The sun was up now and the eastern horizon was a blaze of red gold. The dawn ignited a high bank of clouds that seemed to be building toward something dramatic. He almost hoped that it wouldn't rain and spoil the party. But then he remembered that he was a Hill Country rancher and he never wished against the rain.

High above his head a great blue heron came sailing into the clamorous sky from behind him. She was making for the river. He knew her. Her rook was in the old cottonwood tree at the spring-fed stock tank in the back pasture. In years past there had been many pairs nesting there, but for some reason for the last few years there was only one and she had no mate. Every day she made the transit to the rio and back. She was beautiful, all high and perfect grace. He watched the course of her flight as she plunged down the sky toward the river and he began to hear music echoing off the canyon walls of his memory. And there it was again, the longing, the indelible, almost forgotten longing.

He went out to the Cadillac truck and started it up. He'd only had the Cadillac for a few months. The old Model T had to be cranked and he had to take Daniel with him everywhere. But this miracle of twentieth century engineering had an automatic starter. He thought for a moment about having Daniel saddle his horse, but he knew that he didn't have time to ride there. This way he could be back in time for the party. The new truck jolted through the gate and out onto the caliche road. Thank heaven it wasn't raining. The truck would never make it if it were muddy. He was going to the Narrows and the roads only went half way.

# 44

## FLOOD WATERS

**A**nnie looked around the anteroom of the old gin filled with dust, shadows and cobwebs. "Well this is a creepy old place. What did a cotton gin do anyway? It's something about separating the seeds from the cotton, isn't it?"

Gray said he didn't really know, but he knew they didn't make music. She smiled at his joke and he wondered how anything could be funny after what they'd just come through. They stood together looking out the window at the storm. Gray began to look back over their wild ride and realized how impossibly calm Annie had remained through the entire evening.

"Well isn't this interesting. Just when I thought I couldn't be more surprised, here you two are- my favorite couple." Dewy had come up behind them and was standing there with a rifle aimed in their direction. He was wearing a blazer and neatly pressed slacks and a long-sleeved white shirt. He looked like he was ready to go out to a club.

Annie looked at him and said calmly "You know Dewey, this isn't doing you any good at all. You know that; don't you?"

Dewey grinned strangely and said in a saccharine voice "Why Annie dear, how would you have any idea what is good for me and what isn't? I think that this is going to do me a world of good. Now let's get moving. Just follow along the wall to the right. And welcome to my new home. You arrived just in time for the house warming party."

They moved through the great hall of the building for a hundred feet or so and then came to a metal door. Dewey told Gray to open it and then followed them through it and down a flight of metal stairs and out onto a kind of metal grate catwalk. There was an overhang from the building above their heads. It protected them from the diminishing rain but they looked out on the full fury of the river raging beneath them. Gray wondered how the storm could have quieted so much so fast. Looking at the radar last night, he'd thought that it would be days before it broke, but looking at it now it seemed clear that it was dispersing. Sure Texas weather was weird but this was another thing entirely. They were walking toward the head of the waterfall, only it wasn't there. Usually at this point the river would have poured down through the great wheels that once powered the mill. They were contained within concrete walls but open to the water at the top. They had been silent a long time but now you couldn't even see where they were. The roaring current covered them all.

Dewey herded them down the catwalk until they came to an open archway through which there was a corridor with two doors in it. They both had padlocks on them. He tossed Gray a key ring with one key on it and had him open the first door. Then he ushered them inside. There were two people in the room. One was the big man who had beaten Gray so badly. He was dead. He lay on the concrete floor, his eyes staring.

The other was Beth. She was on a bed tied hand and foot and blindfolded.

Annie said "Oh God, Beth!" She ran to her and sat on the side of the bed and took off her blindfold and pulled a piece of duct tape off of her mouth and hugged her.

Dewey said "Ah reunions, always touching." Annie was tugging at the tape around Beth's wrists. But Dewey said 'Nope, just leave that be, Annie. You'll be joining her soon enough." Then he turned his attention to Gray. "OK asshole, grab the big guy's feet and drag him out of here."

Gray lifted Slomo's legs and began pulling. The dead man was enormous and his body was stiff with rigamortis. Dewey moved into the corner of the room and carried the rifle by the sling hung over his shoulder. He'd taken out a hand gun instead. It took an enormous effort for Gray to pull the corpse out of the room through the door and onto the catwalk. Then, at Dewey's prompting, he pulled it down to the end of the walk. He could only do it in starts and stops, by jerking the load one lunge after another. Dewey followed him out, pausing long enough to lock the padlock of the room on the way.

"There's a gate in the railing at the end" Dewey said. "Open it and push him off."

Gray managed to get the big man's body through the gate and watched as it slid beneath the surface of the river and disappeared. He wondered if it would be carried by the flood all the way to the Gulf of Mexico or if it would hang up along the way and be found by some fisherman and then the police. He wondered if it mattered.

Dewey was standing out on an extension to the side of the main catwalk. It was built to let the workers look directly down into the machinery and inspect for problems. He had traded weapons again and was aiming the deer rifle at Gray's chest. "Well, asshole, now I'm giving you a choice… and a chance if you like. It's not much of a chance but if you get lucky, well, who knows? You can either dive in from where you stand or I'll shoot you and you can fall in. Of course, you'll probably be dead either way so it won't matter much. So what's it going to be?"

Gray knew that he had to try the dive. He looked out on the current and also knew that it was hopeless.

Then he saw it, behind Dewey's back, upriver. A tree was rushing along the wall of the mill. It was big, and black and heavy, with a huge trunk trailing branches where a few dead leaves still clung stubbornly. The root system in the lead extended a good six feet above the water line. As Gray watched it approach, it looked like one of the great threatening monsters that his childhood nightmares created from the shadows on his bedroom walls. He watched as it approached Dewey's perch like a great clawed hand. Just before it struck, Dewey turned to look, following Gray's stare. Before he could react it took the extension where he was standing, catwalk, rails, support struts and all, as cleanly and efficiently as any demolition crew. Dewey was swept away down the flood. While Gray watched in horrified fascination, his enemy surfaced. He caught the branches of the great tree and pulled himself up out of the water as far as his waist. He was facing Gray and he was laughing triumphantly. He raised his arm as high as he could and Gray could see his middle finger extended as he shook it above his head.

Gray thought, "Damn it, he made it. It's not over yet." He wondered, if he called the police whether they could catch Dewy somewhere downriver before he disappeared. He thought it was unlikely with the storm to contend with.

The tree was being swept around the bend in the river, just below the Crossing. Dewey was about to disappear from view. He was climbing higher in the branches, making himself more secure. Suddenly the tree rolled and took him under. Only his hands were visible as he struggled to pull himself up. But the branches that offered him rescue were now his obstacle. He was tangled and as he worked to get free, the tree kept rolling, pulling him under again. He struggled desperately but he couldn't climb and he couldn't free himself. He vanished underwater as the tree rounded the curve and just as it was lost to Gray's view he saw Dewey's hand and the cuff of his white shirt reaching, grasping at the air in the early dawn light. Then there was only the river and its stolen treasures going by- a bright yellow kayak, a set of wooden patio furniture, a beach ball.

Gray had another feeling of déjà vu, the strongest yet. He turned back to the flood. It was terrifying. The river was rising very quickly. It was enormously powerful and the roar kept getting louder. The waterfall was gone, swallowed up completely, all twenty plus feet of it. Even the slight downturn had disappeared as the rising river smoothed over the slight change in elevation. The river was more than twice its normal width. He looked across at his home, the little yellow house where he had spent so many hours of his life. The front door was open. The river was inside above the threshold. It was climbing up the door frame. Things were going to be different now. His world would be different.

His feet were wet. He realized that the water was over the catwalk now and still rising. He began to be afraid for Annie and Beth, still imprisoned in the mill. Then he realized that Dewey had never asked for the key back after he'd opened the door. He was turning to free the women and suddenly it grew quieter. The roar was replaced by her song again, that plaintive, longing melody that had called him from his dreams so many times, but it rose into a roar of its own in symphonic form. It was like standing in the center of the orchestra pit at Carnegie Hall. And then he saw her, across the river. His naked singer was standing at the edge of the flood in the shadows beneath the cypresses, holding night back against the growing dawn. She was totally unaffected by the storm around her. For once he was close enough to see her clearly. She was Annie, well, not Annie, but very like her. It was Annie's face smiling Annie's smile, only so pale that she almost glowed in the dark. She held her hand over her head in greeting or farewell and then she was gone. A blue heron sailed downriver just above the flood waters as if there were no storm. And as he turned back to the door of the tool room, he noticed the rain had stopped.

# 45

## THE IMMORTALS

**W**hen he got to the Narrows the sun was nearing mid-sky. He had to drive carefully around the mesquite and the prickly pear cactus. Either one could leave him with a flat tire. He had found that out the hard way. There was a good breeze blowing out of the south and the mesquite trees around his parking place were filled with cardinals, all singing to him for his birthday. He laughed at his foolishness. Stopping well back from the canyon he got out of the truck and made his slow careful way to the edge and looked down. They told him that he was still spry for his age. He shook his head, spry. Nobody ever says spry about the young, he told himself wryly. It's an old man's word. Ah, well… He looked down into the defile and wished he were a lot spryer. It was sixty or seventy feet deep. The climb down was not difficult, a cakewalk really, at least it was when he was forty-five. At eighty-five he wasn't so sure.

He decided to call her from the top and see if she'd come. He wanted to avoid risking the climb with his bad knee. He'd gone through this ritual several times over the years. But no matter how long he called her she never came and he would climb down. She never came there either but at times he could feel her near, as if she had just left to avoid him, as if she were there somewhere watching. He wanted to call her in; tell her hide and seek was over and they should eat dinner. His hails echoed off the canyon walls but she never answered.

He wished he had on some different boots. Cowboy boots aren't made for climbing rocks, but he hadn't worn anything else in a very long time, not since he'd first come to Texas. He remembered the boots he wore for hiking and climbing when he was young in Germany. He and Henry would hike across the border to Innsbruck and there was a rock there at the foot of the mountain, nearly two hundred feet high and some pretty tough climbing too, and they would scale the thing from different sides and meet at the top and the last one up had to buy the beer that night. It was on top of that rock that Henry had told him he wanted to immigrate to America and asked him to come along. He thought, if they'd known how hard it would be they would have stayed home and waited for the conscription gangs to get them. And it hadn't mattered. They both wound up fighting anyway, Hans with the Union and Henry with the Home Guard against the Comanche, and both of them against the Texicans. You can't hide from destiny. Life teaches everyone the same lessons. Then he laughed. He went to Texas and fought against slavery and Indians and outlaws and made love to a goddess. Now that is a destiny!

He started into the defile cautiously, making sure of each foothold. Looking downstream to make sure he was in the right place, he saw a blue heron. He wondered if it could be the same one he'd seen fly over his head this morning at the ranch. He'd have to ask her. And then he was falling. The rock beneath his right foot suddenly shifted and he was sliding and bouncing and then tumbling head over heels to the bottom.

He lay on the limestone floor beside the water. And he thought, "Well, that wasn't so bad" and then he took a deep breath and a sharp pain rattled through him and made him gasp. He thought, "Oh oh" and shook his head to clear it. Then he braced his arms to try sitting up, but the pain came so viciously that he nearly lost consciousness. And then she was there, stroking his hair and smiling so tenderly it broke his heart. The pain was gone. He was in her arms and she was cradling him in her lap and singing to him, that lullaby from so long ago.

"Shush shush, my darling. Everything is just fine." And she kept singing and she kept stroking his hair and kissing him, his forehead and his lips. Holding him. Just holding him…

"Where have you been?" He asked her. "I called you so many times. You never came. I could feel you there. Why didn't you answer me? You never answered me."

"I didn't understand about humans yet, my love. But I do now. I do. Don't worry. We'll have a whole life together next time. You'll see."

"No, we missed our chance. It's too late. I'm leaving. I feel it."

"Ah my darling, that's the surprise. You won't die. You will close your eyes and go to sleep. And then you will wake up and start over. And after a little I'll be there and we will love each other and we'll have music and we'll sing together and maybe we will have a child. I'm not sure. But it will be wonderful. You'll see."

He said, "What is your name? You never told me your name."

"I have a lot of names, love" she said, almost in a whisper, "But you can call me Annie."

He smiled at her and she kissed him on the mouth and his eyelids slowly closed and he was asleep.

# EPILOGUE

So, if you go looking for Blue Heron Crossing, remember to take the river. If you follow that map you bought, riding the Texas highways, you'll just get yourself lost. Oh, you may eventually find Morningstar. It's still there, still waiting for the real estate moguls and their big ideas on capitalization and creative enhancement. Someday they'll get there, if the stray lightning bolt or the straying bottle rocket doesn't get there first. But, while you may find the town, and its cemetery, and the low water bridge, you won't find Blue Heron Crossing. The little house, screened with Georgia cane and fronted by a grape arbor, is gone. Panels of corrugated metal siding, still baring traces of yellow paint, are buried in the mud, or roof some small garage or shed along cypress-lined banks, across half of south Texas. Some might even have made it all the way to the Gulf of Mexico, where they'll be dredged up by the pogey boats, or oyster boats, or just left forever, to corrode in the deep and salty sea. But if you refuse to follow maps, if you resent the encroaching developers and long desperately to leave them and their shabby enhancements behind, do what I tell you. Go by way of the River. Hear her songs. Listen to their echoes. The River may only go where she has to go and she may always get there, but on the River, time is meaningless. She wanders where she has to, but she gets there when she wants to. And if you are handsome and sensitive and young, or passionate, strong, and brave, she may take you with her. If she does, you'll have a wonderful ride. And you might even wind up at Blue Heron Crossing, watching a heron winging away south, high and fast and disappearing into a dream.

\*\*\*